# HELLBOUND

## Hellbound Series Book 1

Written by Sara Clancy
Edited by David Longhorn and Merill Ravago

ISBN: 9798469860211
Copyright © 2021 by ScareStreet.com

All rights reserved. This book or any portion thereof may not be reproduced or used in any manner whatsoever without written permission from the publisher except for the use of brief quotations in a book review.

*This is a work of fiction. Any resemblance to actual persons, living or dead, or actual events is purely coincidental.*

# Thank You and Bonus Novel!

I'd like to take a moment to thank you for your ongoing support. You make this all possible! To really show you my appreciation for downloading this book, **I'd love to send you a full-length horror novel in 3 formats (MOBI, EPUB and PDF) absolutely free!**

Download your full-length horror novel, get free short stories, and receive future discounts by visiting www.ScareStreet.com/SaraClancy

See you in the shadows,
Sara Clancy

# Chapter 1

Wren stopped fussing with his party hat when Lark shot him a warning glare. Pulled stubble was easier to deal with than an angry sister.

"I can't light the candles if you don't hold it still," Shrike said for the third time.

Lark squirmed like an excited toddler but managed to keep the cake somewhat steady. With nothing to do but wait, Wren mindlessly glanced around the corridor. Caught between Christmas and New Year, the airport motor inn had a steady stream of guests. It was cheap but pleasant. Like every other motel they had stayed at over the years.

Movement flashed across the corner of his eye. He turned. The door to the last room before the staircase was open, allowing a dark shadow to spill out into the hall. A perfect silhouette of a man with a flat brimmed hat. The shadow never moved. Whoever cast it stayed in the room, just out of sight.

"I think that guy's waiting for us to leave," he told his sisters.

Shrike grunted.

"Dad is going to love these guys." Lark beamed at the fondant cardinals that topped the birthday cake. "Aren't they just the cutest things?"

"You're going to drop it." Shrike moved the lighter to the last unlit candle.

"No, I won't! You always do this. You know—"

Wren knew that telltale squeak in his little sister's voice that promised an endless flood of words.

"Still breathing?" Wren asked.

On reflex, all three siblings splayed a hand across their chests and drew in a slow, deep breath. Their father had used the simple trick to cut off all sorts of childhood meltdowns and it was still affective. One by one, they calmly confirmed.

"Still breathing."

Lark sighed. "I'm just excited that we managed to find such a perfect cake."

"We didn't find it," Wren said. "I ordered it."

"Same thing."

Wren huffed. "It's really not. And if this save hadn't taken so long, we would have been able to do all the other stuff I had planned."

"Dad will be happy with just a quiet night in," Shrike said.

"Just him and his favorite kid," Lark said. "Oh, and you two."

Wren scoffed. "I'm his first born and only son. Clearly I'm the favorite."

"Everyone knows the baby is always the favorite," Lark countered.

"That's all you guys got? Genetic accidents?" Shrike flicked her Zippo closed and returned it to its designated pocket in her cargo pants. "Dad likes me for my personality. I win. Now give me the cake."

"I'm holding the cake," Lark said.

Wren readjusted his glasses, making the hat strap snag his stubble again. "Lark, you're thirty-five. You're too old to pout."

"My face muscles disagree with you." She exaggerated the expression to prove the point.

After an argument that the surrounding rooms would have heard, the siblings crowded together, each keeping a hand on the cake tray as they began to sing.

"Happy birthday to you."

Wren fumbled one-handed with the lock.

"Happy birthday to you."

The latch finally gave and he kicked the door open.

"Happy birthday, dear—" Wren's throat swelled shut.

His stomach lurched as the world seemed to fall apart around him. The only thing that remained still was the pile of mangled flesh heaped in the center of the room.

"Daddy?" Lark whimpered.

The cake slipped from their fingers, the colorful icing splattering across the blood-soaked carpet. In unison, the siblings ran across the ransacked room, sprinting to their father's lifeless body.

\*\*\*

Shrike nudged the toe of her boot into the crack that severed a white tile. Muffled wails and the scent of disinfectant wafted out through the mental ward's heavy doors. She had anticipated the order and simplicity. But the wall of huge, heavily barred windows and the garden that lay beyond caught her off guard. The place was unnervingly pleasant. Resting her elbows on her thighs, she absently pushed her long bangs back from her face. Her fingers snagged on the mass of knotted, frizzy curls. She had forgotten to gel it down again. Ripping her hands free, she slumped back in the plastic seat and stared up at the ceiling. They hadn't taken down the Christmas decorations yet.

"Have you found anything new?" Lark asked.

Shrike turned her attention to Wren, who had taken the chair nearest the power outlet. Hunched over his laptop, he pushed his glasses up the bridge of his nose and continued to ignore everything else around him.

"Wren?" Shrike pressed. "Wren!"

He flinched and snapped his head up. "What?"

"Lark wanted an update on the research."

"Oh." Wren pulled his glasses off and rubbed at the bags under his eyes.

"Something must have happened to her. Something horrible. Lisa was so normal before we saved her. She wasn't capable of doing—" Lark hugged her knees to her chest and fell silent.

"She went to ground days after we saved her," Wren said. "Her social media went quiet. Her friends and relatives haven't heard from her. I even tracked down her work and they said she just left mid-shift and they haven't seen her since. It's like she woke up one day and decided to leave her whole life behind."

Shrike brushed her bangs back again. "It sounds like she was hiding from someone. A stalker maybe?"

"It's possible. But shouldn't we have noticed someone else following her?" Wren asked.

"Maybe she joined a cult. Like the Manson Family," Lark suggested. "Or she might have gone insane. Or alien invasion—"

"Alien invasion?" Shrike raised an eyebrow.

"Maybe. Like *Invasion of the Body Snatchers*. Or *The Thing*."

"This isn't a movie, Lark!"

"Still breathing?" Wren cut in.

The argument stalled as muscle memory took over. Each sibling placed a hand on their chests, drawing in a slow, deep breath. Wren flicked his attention between his siblings.

"Still breathing," he prompted.

Lark sniffed. "Still breathing."

"Dad's never going to ask that question again." Shrike dropped her hand onto her lap and hung her head. Everything hurt. A physical, bone deep ache. "Still breathing."

"Good. No more arguing," Wren mumbled.

Shrike cracked her knuckles as a now familiar rage bubbled in her chest. "I'm going to kill that—"

"Shrike." Wren's voice was soft but full of warning.

Clenching her jaw until her teeth ached, she growled. "Dad saved her life and she butchered him. She deserves—"

"Stop." Wren looked deliberately at the nurse's station. The orderlies chatted with each other and shuffled papers. "It took a lot to get this meeting. We can't give them an excuse to keep us from Lisa."

"I don't understand," Lark whispered. "Dad could see death. Why didn't he see this coming?"

Wren shrugged. "Dad could only foresee *accidental* death. This was murder."

"Whatever makes him see these things could have bent the rules just this once," Lark pressed.

"Maybe it didn't know." Shrike clutched her hands together, ignoring her hair as it fell into her eyes again. "All these years and we still have no idea how Dad's visions worked. There was never any pattern."

"Except that they were always accidents," Wren stressed.

"Except that," Shrike agreed.

Lark hummed; her eyes fixed on the wedding bands she held. She twisted them back and forth, making the gold catch the light.

"Dad once told me that he thought Mom was sending the visions," Lark whispered. "He said that she saw how devastated we were to lose her, and she wanted to save other families from going through that."

"It's possible," Wren said.

"I think it's her," Lark said. "That's just the kind of thing Mom would do."

Shrike didn't answer. Lark had only been two years old when their mother died in a car accident. Her 'memories' were a patchwork of things Dad had told her, and stories she had made up herself. Shrike could barely recall their mother, and she didn't like trying to. Amongst all the smiles and laughter was a lingering shadow of fear.

"Are you guys sure it's okay for me to keep the rings?" Lark asked.

Pulled from her thoughts, Shrike mumbled, "Yeah, go ahead."

"I don't mind," Wren added.

"You know, I remember Mom wearing this," Lark said. "I remember she used to squeeze my hand whenever I stumbled, trying to keep me from falling, and the ring would hurt just a little."

Shrike glanced at Wren. He was already looking at her over the rim of his glasses, his fingers flying over the keyboard. After a few looks that amounted to them mentally screaming 'not it', Shrike heaved a sigh. It took her a second to come up with the foundations of a lie her sister could have fun building upon.

"You used to play with her ring," she said.

"I did?" Lark asked.

"Yeah. Um, Mom would read us bedtime stories, but you would get bored and start fiddling with the diamond."

Lark's face brightened. "I remember that. I thought it was so pretty."

Shrike tuned out her sister's steady flow of words. With time and repetition, Lark would dress up the lie until it was indistinguishable from the truth. Their mother never read to them. That was Dad's thing. But Lark was smiling for the first time in days and neither sibling was going to ruin that.

Shrike couldn't pinpoint what alerted her, but she leapt to her feet and squared off with the end of the corridor. Seconds passed and she realized how dim the nurse's station had grown. The few staff there continued to work, unconcerned with the darkness that washed over their sealed booth. It moved like a shadow but there was a strange density to it. She glanced over her shoulder. Wren was hunched over his laptop while Lark regaled him with her developing story. It felt like she was the only one who even noticed that something was off. Turning back, Shrike cursed sharply. That got her sibling's attention. In a smooth motion, Lark unfurled from her seat, slipped across the corridor, and took the chair beside Wren.

Shrike backed up a step to close ranks with her siblings. Tall and muscular, she became a wall separating them from the approaching uniformed officer.

"What the hell is he doing here?" Shrike muttered. "Anyone remember his name?"

"Officer Barsotti," Lark supplied.

"He's out of his jurisdiction," Wren said.

"How sure are you about that?" Shrike asked.

Wren dropped his voice as the officer came closer. "He's a low ranked highway patrol officer. It seems unlikely that he'd be in a mental ward in an official capacity."

They fell silent as the officer came into earshot.

"Hello, Rose siblings." He started to go around Shrike.

She cut him off, forcing him to keep his distance from the others. He was a tall man but, at six-foot-three, she still had a good couple of inches on him. And a lot more muscle. An amused smile spread across his face. It stayed even after he winced and dabbed his thumb against his cut lip.

"Hi, Officer Barsotti," Lark chirped.

He tipped to the side to look around Shrike. "You can call me Barsotti."

"Your eye looks horrible, Barsotti," Lark said sweetly. "Probably should have put some ice on that."

"I did. Your sister just has one hell of a right hook. I was hoping we could have a quick conversation."

"It's a bad time," Shrike said coldly.

"I don't think there's going to be a good one," Barsotti said. "Given the circumstances."

"If you leave your card with us, we'll give you a call in a few days," Wren said.

Barsotti clicked his tongue. "And risk you forgetting about me before you head off? You lot never seem to stay in one place very long. And you're far from home. You're from Colorado, right?"

Shrike grabbed Barsotti's shoulder and shoved him upright, once again blocking his view to her siblings. "You've looked into us?"

"Standard procedure."

"For a random murder?"

"Might not be so random," he countered.

Shrike clenched her jaw. "I was about to do a coffee run. You can ask your questions on the way to the vending machine."

Barsotti considered her for a long moment. Eventually, he stepped aside and swept a hand down the hallway. She didn't move. Barsotti huffed a laugh and rubbed the edges of his black eye. He took a step and Shrike followed. They remained silent until they had passed by the nurse's station and started down the next corridor.

"So, you and your siblings." Barsotti paused to look her over. "You're all genetically related?"

"How is that relevant?"

"It's not. Just making conversation."

Shrike glanced at him before scanning the barren walls. There was nowhere to hide. But also nowhere for her to go if this was an ambush.

"They look like Dad. I take after our mother's side."

"Your mother—"

"Is not relevant," she cut him off. "Why are you here? They caught the person who killed Dad. There's nothing more for you to do."

"As the first one on the scene, I feel rather attached." When she didn't respond, he pulled his phone out of his pocket and fiddled with the settings. "And there's a few things that just need clearing up. For paperwork and all that."

He held up his phone, showing her a long-distance picture of a woman. Shrike recognized her instantly as one of their latest saves. Her stomach clenched.

"We checked his camera's memory card. He had a lot of photos like this. Any idea why?"

Shrike glanced at the picture. "She's a beautiful specimen."

"You don't have any issue with him taking creeper shots of strangers?"

"It's a bird."

Barsotti frowned and looked down at his screen. "The pigeon? You want me to believe that your dad took a dozen shots of a pigeon and this woman just happened to be in the background?"

"Yes."

"He took photos of a *pigeon*."

"Dad was an avid birdwatcher, and we don't have a lot of that particular breed back home."

"That's your story?"

"It's not a story. It's the truth."

"Come on," he urged. "Do you think anyone is going to believe that?"

"The man named all of his children after birds. Clearly, he was a little obsessed," Shrike said.

Barsotti smirked and pulled a hand through his soft brown hair. "You've got me there. And the binoculars?"

She studied him carefully as they neared the vending machines. "They're essential for birdwatching. Obviously."

"Of course. But you must see how, combined with his telescopic camera, the photographs, the maps of urban neighborhoods; well, it seems like a stalker kit."

"You have to stalk birds to watch them."

She jabbed at the buttons on the coffee machine, not paying attention to what she was ordering. Wren would drink anything with caffeine at this point. Barsotti hummed noncommittedly and leaned a shoulder against the wall. Anger simmered in her chest as he watched her with that damn smirk still on his face. She took deep, soothing breaths but felt her control slipping.

"You know, I'm being awfully nice to you. You should be a little more grateful and a lot more cooperative."

Shrike laughed. "Nice?"

"You assaulted a police officer," he reminded her.

She glared at him as the machine started to whirl. "You put your hands on my sister."

"She was contaminating a crime scene."

"She was hugging our father!"

Chest heaving and fists balled, she closed the minimal distance separating them.

"You've got quite the temper on you," Barsotti said calmly. "And a nasty habit of assault. Like that incident with Lisa—"

"How do you know about that?"

"Fun fact, when charges are dropped, we don't incinerate all the paperwork and lobotomize everyone involved. There's always a trail."

"I was giving her CPR. Her friends were drunk. They

misunderstood. The moment they were sober, they realized their mistake and let it go."

"Funny how you happened to be there, though. At a private wedding in a restricted resort."

Shrike drew in a deep breath and forced her fingers to relax. "Still breathing."

"What?" Barsotti asked.

"Nothing. Look, that all happened over a year ago."

"Two-year statute of limitation on trespassing."

"Then charge me or get the hell out of my way."

Until that moment, Shrike had never known that a single expression could be so utterly condescending. Barsotti smiled and pointed one finger to the machine.

"Your coffee's ready."

She clenched her jaw so hard her teeth threatened to crack. Wrenching the paper cup out from the little compartment made the coffee slosh over her hand, the burn adding to her anger rather than tapering it. Barsotti frowned at her reddening skin.

"Why are you here?" she snapped.

"Your father—"

"You're a traffic cop! Shouldn't the lead detective be doing this?"

Barsotti stiffened. "You looked into that? Huh."

"You hold our father's body hostage and—"

"No," he cut in. "You can't blame me for that. Bodies are always held during ongoing investigations."

"What investigation? The woman that killed him is in that room!"

"Yeah, I know. Don't forget that I'm the one that helped arrange this little get together. Oh? You didn't know that? Yeah. I pulled a few strings and now you owe a couple of favors. You're welcome, by the way."

Shrike stared at him. "Why would you do that?"

He finally dropped the smile. "There's some things you can't leave behind when you clock out at the end of the day." After a moment of silence, he shook himself and his confident smirk returned. "Besides, I've got this feeling that just won't let me sleep."

"A 'feeling' about what, exactly?"

She studied him. There was no way to tell exactly what he was thinking, but the prospect that he was contemplating something, working the pieces until they fit, put her on edge. For the first time, Dad wouldn't be able to guide them through it. There was an undefinable shift in Barsotti. He didn't seem so obnoxious anymore. He seemed competent and insightful. An actual threat.

"That night," he began. "I thought I saw something."

"Something? What are you talking about?"

"Shrike!"

At Lark's cry, Shrike tossed the cup aside and sprinted back down the corridor. She caught a fleeting glimpse of a motionless, dark figure looming behind the startled nurses before she skidded around the corner. Then the only thing she cared about was the huge men flanking her little sister.

"It's alright," Wren said as he shoved his laptop into its carry satchel. "They've just come to tell us they're ready. We can see Lisa now."

# Chapter 2

Surrounded by the guards and her sister, Lark could barely glimpse the tiny, stark white room. The air conditioner produced a steady low hum, a backdrop to the squeak of chair legs and measured breaths. She glanced behind and found Wren crowding closer. He clutched at the front of his jacket, already missing the satchel that they had insisted he keep outside. Wren offered her a reassuring smile as the door slammed shut and locked with a buzz. Now that they were sealed inside, it was like the temperature had plummeted. Lark's fingers and toes pricked with the cold. The guards moved to take their positions along the walls, and she was finally able to see the woman who had murdered her father.

Lisa had been forcibly medicated after her arrest and wasn't present for most of the legal proceedings the siblings had managed to sit in on. Lark had fond memories of Lisa. The woman had been sociable and bold. Even stalking her had been fun. She barely recognized the woman shackled to the narrow metal table. Dark regrowth streaked her once carefully bleached hair. Her lips were pale and chapped, her eyes sunken and red. Her once perfect skin had sagged and collapsed into her cheek hollows. It was like she had aged decades in the single year they had left her. Sinking into one of the chairs set opposite her, Lark followed the woman's fixed gaze to the barred window. It had started to snow.

"They're thinking it's going to storm later tonight," Lark said.

Lark loved idle chit-chat. She specifically liked how people would always reveal more than they ever intended once they were good and comfortable. Lisa didn't take the bait.

"Are they treating you well?" Lark asked gently. "You look a little pale."

The show of compassion had Shrike squirming on the edges of Lark's peripheral vision. Wren, having taken the offered seat, did a better job at hiding his annoyance. Neither of them had ever perfected their poker faces.

"Lisa," Lark said. "We just want to understand why you did what you did."

The fat snowflakes falling past the window cast shadows over the walls. The instant Lisa finally met her gaze, Lark was sure those dancing spots congealed into the silhouette of a man. A tall man, with broad shoulders and a flat brimmed hat. She blinked and the illusion was gone.

"He wouldn't stop." Lisa's voice was rough. Like every word hurt. "I had to."

"Wouldn't stop what?" Barsotti asked.

There was malice in Barsotti's tone that almost made Lark whirl on him.

"Our father wasn't capable of hurting anyone," Wren said.

"I'd like to hear what Lisa has to say," Barsotti replied.

Lisa had kept her eyes fixed on Lark.

"They weren't supposed to live," Lisa whispered.

"You mean the people that Dad saved?" Remembering Barsotti and the guards, Lark quickly added. "Dad has a knack for being in the right place at the right time. He had helped a lot of people."

"People like you," Wren said.

"He saved you and you did this to him," Shrike snarled.

Tears welled in Lisa's eyes and darkness gathered behind her. "He didn't save me. He condemned me."

"What?" Lark hurriedly motioned for her siblings to keep quiet. "Help me understand. A greater force wanted you alive and—"

Everyone flinched as Lisa threw herself against the table, but the woman only saw Lark.

"It was a demon," she hurriedly whispered. "Don't you see? It wasn't a benevolent angel whispering in your father's ear. It was a demon."

"We might need to cut this short," a guard said.

Lark ignored the man and the warnings to keep her distance as she inched a little closer to Lisa.

"Why would a demon want to save people?"

"Because we're marked for possession. Two days after you saved me, a demon burrowed its way inside." Lisa's voice dropped to a whimper. "It's still inside me."

"No—"

"It was all a trick, Lark. Your father never *saved* anyone. He was just keeping us alive long enough to be hosts. I had to stop him."

"Okay," a guard said. "She's getting a little worked up. Let's give her some time to rest. We can try again another time."

"It's a nightmare. I've never been this cold. It hurts." Tears dripped from Lisa's eyes. "I can feel it eating me from the inside. Do you know what it's like to be devoured alive? And I can't get it out of me. Joe had to be stopped before he did this to anyone else. I didn't want to hurt him. It was only supposed to be one hit. Who survives an ax to the head? Just one strike and it would be done. Almost painless. But he kept moving. I told him to stop. I told him to stay still. But he kept moving. He wouldn't die."

Lisa pulled against her restraints and clutched Lark's hand. Her skin was like ice.

"Lisa," one of the guards said, calm but stern. "You have to let her go now."

Lark couldn't stop the images from flooding her brain. She tried to pull away and Lisa tightened her grip. "Let me go."

"We have to finish it," Lisa said.

The guards had already closed in around them and were gently trying to pry the women apart, careful not to provoke an outburst. Lisa sunk her nails into Lark's forearm. The cold deepened until Lark began to shake.

"You have to make sure we die," Lisa insisted. "Just like we were supposed to."

The guards gave up on being tactful. One looped a beefy arm around Lisa's shoulders and yanked her back, pinning her small frame to the chair. Another tried to pull Lisa's hand off Lark. Shrike moved forward to help, and Lisa screamed. The sound was feral and strained and entirely inhuman. Lisa threw herself back, tossing the men aside as she lurched to her feet. One yank and the thick chain shackling her to the table snapped. Lisa threw herself at Lark, and Shrike surged forward. Muscles bunching, Shrike grabbed the raging woman around the neck and drove her down against the table. Shadows swirled over the walls and the air became bitterly cold. The guards tried to pin her down but Lisa broke free again. She clung to Shrike and bit at the tender flesh of her neck. Blood spurted across the white floor.

"Get out," Barsotti shoved Lark into Wren and ordered them both from the room.

There was a guard with them before they could protest. Barsotti charged toward the chaos, blocking Lark's view of her struggling sister. Then they were thrown into the hall and the door slammed shut. Nurses rushed down the corridor. Most of them went inside while one stayed to usher the siblings back into the waiting room.

Lisa's screams followed them. "You have to undo what you did! We were supposed to die! You have to kill us all!"

\*\*\*

Their new motor inn loved pastel blue but never used the exact same shade twice. Wren had claimed the queen bed by the window. He was surprised to glance out it now and find that the sun had long since set. The predicted snowstorm was in full force. A few stray cars passed by on their way to the airport, but it seemed that most had decided to take the subway instead. It rumbled past, undisturbed by the gathering ice. He chastised himself for letting so much time slip by unnoticed. Hiding away wasn't an option anymore. Their father was gone. His sisters needed him present.

"Maybe we should order some dinner." He pushed his glasses up his nose and glanced to the other bed.

Shrike and Lark were staring at him, both frozen mid-bite of their pork buns, a half dozen Chinese takeout containers scattered around them.

"Yeah," Lark swallowed. "That seems like an awesome idea, bro. And we'd totally wait for you before we ate."

"We got you some fried rice." Shrike handed him a box. the motion pulled at the stitches on her neck and made her wince.

"Take the painkillers," Lark said.

"I don't like them," Shrike said.

"Come on. They're 'please don't sue us' drugs. Those are the best kind."

"You know they give me nightmares. I'm having bad enough dreams already."

All the life melted from Lark's face. She stabbed absently at her food with a plastic fork.

"I don't think any of us are sleeping well," she mumbled.

"Why don't you take a half dose?" Wren offered. "I'll wake you up if you get restless. I'll pay attention, I promise."

Shrike had never been able to hold her ground against both siblings. With an annoyed grunt, she shuffled off the bed to rummage through her cargo pants pockets.

"So, what have you been looking at this whole time?" Lark asked.

"Oh, um," Wren stammered. He looked to his laptop screen. A half dozen open windows of different demonic lore. "Nothing, really. Just more Lisa stuff. Why? Is there something you want me to check out?"

"No." Lark speared a shrimp.

The siblings fell silent. Shrike had found the small bottle and rattled it between her hands.

"I can't stop thinking about what Lisa said," Shrike blurted out. "I know, it's crazy."

"I can't either!" Lark said.

"And it's not that crazy, when you think about it," Wren said. "I mean, we know so little about Dad's visions and what caused them. We just assumed that it came from something good."

Lark curled up and rested the takeout container on her knees. "Do you really think a demon could trick Dad?" Lark asked.

"He wasn't infallible," Shrike said.

"He was close," Lark mumbled.

"I'm struggling to wrap my head around the concept that demons are real," Shrike said. "I mean, it's one thing to follow Dad's lead. But *demons*. That's a huge leap. I'm not sure if I'm ready to jump."

Lark jabbed at her food. "Okay, you have to promise not to laugh at me."

"Why?" Wren asked.

Lark shot him a look and refused to say another word until both of her older siblings had verbally promised.

"Okay, well, back at the hospital, when we were talking to Lisa, I think I saw something."

"Something?" Wren pressed.

"A shadow. But like, a man's shadow. With a hat." Lark groaned. "I'm not explaining this well."

"I saw it too," Shrike said.

"You did?" Lark and Wren asked in unison.

"Yeah. In the hallway. I'm sure someone was just passing by."

"No, I saw it behind her in the room. Before she started talking," Lark said.

Shrike stared at her for a moment before huffing and dragged her hands through her matted hair. "This is ridiculous. We are literally jumping at shadows."

"I might have done a bit of research," Wren admitted.

"Shocking," Lark mumbled.

He ignored her. "The concept of a 'shadow demon' or 'shadow people' keeps coming up. There's one that's commonly seen. They generally refer to him as Hat Man." Enlarging one of the pictures, he spun the screen around to face them.

Lark squealed before he could ask if there was any similarity.

"That's it! That's what I saw! Shrike, what about you?"

Shrike gaped at the screen.

"Shrike?" Lark pressed.

"I only saw it for a second."

"Yeah, me too. But I know what I saw." Lark hunched her shoulders and lowered her voice. "It kinda stuck in my head."

Wren shot Shrike a questioning look.

"That's what I saw." She avoided his gaze and dry swallowed one of the pills. "What else did you find?"

"A lot. It seems like every culture since the dawn of time has had some take on the concept of demons. I have no way to gauge what information is accurate."

"What if we looked into the people Dad saved?" Lark said. "If they are getting possessed, then maybe there'll be a common theme."

Wren nodded. "I thought of that, but honestly couldn't remember all their names. I don't suppose either of you kept a list."

"Dad always said it didn't seem right," Lark said.

Shrike sat back down on the mattress and pulled out her phone. "Okay. Tell me who you remember."

It was a slow process. Events, faces, and stray bits of information were a lot easier to recall than actual names. The food went cold as they struggled back through the years, trying not to be drawn into memories that hurt too much to think about.

"Okay, that'll be enough for now." Wren hovered his fingers over his laptop keys. "Give me the first name."

"Amanda Wilson."

Lark ate a mouthful of cold rice. "She was the one that dressed up as a fairy, right?"

"For children's birthday parties," Shrike confirmed.

Wren quickly scanned through the search results, not believing it until he found a news report with an attached photograph.

"She's dead."

"When? How?" Lark asked in rapid succession.

"A few years ago. Suicide."

"Suicide?" Shrike repeated.

"She wasn't suicidal when we followed her, was she?" Lark asked. "I'm sure I would remember if the fairy was suicidal."

"I can't remember," Wren said.

Shrike shrugged. "They've all blurred together. Wren, how did she do it?"

"She jumped off a bridge overpass onto a motorway." He read a few more lines and groaned. "Oh, damn it. She did it during rush hour and caused a five-car pile-up."

"That's awful," Lark said.

"But not conclusively demonic," Shrike added. "Next name. Francis O'Reilly."

"The manager at Blockbuster Videos. Now I feel old." Again, Wren just needed a simple internet search to produce a flood of results. "Oh."

"Please, tell me that he's not dead," Lark said.

"He's doing a life sentence. He took a gun to work, locked staff and patrons inside and, well, they don't go into detail."

"Oh God," Lark said. "But he was so nice. I remember him giving me popcorn."

"Amelia Kennedy," Shrike said.

"Who?" Lark asked.

"College student," Shrike said.

A quick search and his stomach went cold. Wren pulled his glasses off and rubbed his dry eyes. "She's missing."

Shrike reached over and turned the laptop around.

"I remember the date of this save," she said. "Amelia was reported missing three days after we intervened."

"Okay, I'm officially worried that we've really messed up," Lark said.

"I'm sure there's a reasonable explanation," Shrike assured.

Lark said. "Search for the one we just helped. The bus driver. Arkansas, that's it. Trent Arkansas."

Wren hurriedly put his glasses back on, and a dark shape caught his attention. He turned to the window. Someone was standing in the well-lit parking lot. The man wasn't rushing to get out of the cold. He simply stood there, staring up at the motel. The hair on the back of Wren's neck prickled.

"Wren?" Shrike asked.

He didn't dare look away from the shape. "I think someone is out there."

"Where?" Lark crawled onto his bed.

"Third lamppost from the right."

"I can't really see," Lark said. "But it's too narrow to be a car."

Shrike tossed Wren's laptop onto the end of his bed, grabbed her jacket, and shoved her feet into her snow boots.

"Lock the door after I leave," she ordered.

Lark forced a laugh, "I'm not letting you go and chase a demon. Are you nuts?"

"We have no evidence that it's a demon," Shrike said.

"We have no evidence that it's not!" Lark snapped.

"Guys," Wren said. "It's gone."

Wren got up and inched closer to the window, trying to see as much of the parking lot as he could. There was only snow and shadows. He pulled the curtains closed. He still felt like someone or something was watching him.

"What happened to Trent?" he asked.

"Nothing came up," Shrike said.

Wren rechecked the locks. "I want to check on him tomorrow."

# Chapter 3

Shrike pulled the hood of her snow coat up. It did nothing against the chill creeping across the back of her neck. No matter how many people crammed onto the crosstown bus, it never seemed to get any warmer. Despite the cold, her neck still throbbed, the pain spiking every time her scarf snagged on the stitches. She readjusted the material with growing irritation as the bus made its way through the city streets. They pulled up to the curb and Shrike tightened her grip on the handrail. The new flow of people coming and going allowed her to shuffle a little closer to her siblings. She flopped into the seat behind Lark.

"My feet have gone numb," Lark whispered. "Can't he turn up the heater?"

More people left and Wren slipped gracefully into the chair in front of his sisters. "I need a coffee."

"Because you're cold or tired?" Lark asked.

He didn't turn around. "Both."

"Me too," Lark sighed. "I kept having weird dreams."

"I feel you," Shrike said.

Lark glanced over her shoulder. "The half dose didn't help?"

"I was able to wake up from the nightmares. So that's an improvement, I guess."

Shrike was relieved when the bus pulled from the curb while there was still a little elbow room. She tried to rearrange her scarf but there was no way to make it comfortable.

"How much longer, do you think?" Shrike asked, eyeing the bus driver in the large rearview mirror. "We've followed him all day and he hasn't done anything strange or violent. He seems the exact same as he was when we last checked in on him."

"He was the easiest save we've ever had," Lark said.

Wren leaned against the window. "We're almost at the end of the line."

"We're lucky he hasn't recognized us yet. It makes it a lot easier to follow him." Lark stomped her feet to try to work some warmth into her toes. After making sure no one was paying attention, she added, "Is anyone else worried that we're being played? What if Lisa's lying? What if Dad was doing the right thing and these bad guys are trying to stop us?"

Shrike grunted. "If that was their goal, they've already achieved it. Dad was the only one who ever knew what was going to happen. He's gone."

"Lisa said that we need to—," Wren cut himself off, glanced around, and rechose his words. "She was specific about what she wanted us to do. That could be their end goal."

Shrike scanned the bus and noticed a passenger watching them. She cleared her throat and they fell silent. Wren and Lark pulled out their phones while Shrike tried not to glare at the intruder. The touch screen didn't work with her gloves. Her fingers were going to freeze to keep this conversation going. Her phone buzzed over and over, and she bitterly pulled off one glove. Her fingertips were numb by the time she managed to yank her still buzzing phone free.

"Guys, give me a second," she muttered under her breath.

Only Lark was close enough to hear her. "It ain't me."

Shrike frowned at the unknown number displayed on the screen. She quickly answered it and shoved her ungloved hand into her pocket. "Hello?"

"Shrike Rose?"

"Barsotti? How did you get this number?"

"Perks of being a police officer," he said. "How's the neck?"

Her eyes drifted back across the aisle. It wasn't just the man watching her now. The woman seated beside him was also staring directly at the siblings.

"Alright, don't answer," Barsotti said. "I was just being polite, anyway. I have a few follow up questions about yesterday."

Shrike watched as the people seated around the couple slowly turned to face her.

"Get someone actually involved in the case to ask me." She hung up and quickly sent a message on the group chat.

*I see them,* Wren replied.

*Three in front,* Lark posted.

Shrike glanced up from her phone to find three people all crowded by the front exit watching them. They didn't talk or move. Just watched. The bus rocked as they took a tight bend. People began to gather their belongings, swirling around the motionless observers. Shrike swayed as the bus jerked to a stop.

"End of the line," Trent bellowed.

The doors swung open, and the tension snapped. All those that had been watching them started toward the door, chatting in small groups, and never looking back. The siblings lingered, letting everyone shuffle out into the winter air, putting some distance between them and the watchers.

Lark forced a smile. "We're just being paranoid, right?"

"No," Wren said. "Those people were watching us."

"We're leaving." Shrike ignored another incoming call and shoved her phone back into her pocket.

The bus had already cleared out, but they were far from alone. The bus depot was a transportation hub, sharing the building with a subway station and intercity buses. All the buses that weren't in use were parked in long neat rows beside the main building, surrounded by a tall chain-link fence. People braved the cold to sneak one last cigarette before continuing their trips. Shrike caught a glimpse of a subway train pulling in and hoped it was the one they needed. She wanted to get back to the motel and out of the cold.

"Hey," Trent called. He twisted around in the driver's seat to smile at them. "You lot look familiar. Have we met?"

"No, I don't think so," Lark dismissed with a smile. "Well, thank you for the lift. Bye."

Trent's warm smile didn't quite reach his eyes. "I'll be seeing you."

The siblings each mumbled their thanks and hurried off the bus. Despite the snow, it was considerably warmer outside. Shrike pushed down her hood, her gaze absently drawn back over her shoulder. Trent was staring at them through the bus driver's window. Meeting her gaze, the man waved, and pulled the empty bus away from the curb. A dark figure loomed in one of the passing windows. She spun around, trying to catch sight of it again. The vehicle passed through a gate into the parking area and was soon lost amongst the rows of buses.

"Did either of you see that?" Shrike asked.

"The shadow man?" Lark whispered. "Yeah, I saw it."

"Come on, the train is about to leave," Wren said.

The sisters turned to him.

"You want us to just leave him alone with it? What if today is the day it possesses him?" Lark asked.

"What if it is?" Wren demanded. "What do you suggest we do about it?"

"Stopping it seems like the appropriate thing to do," Lark shot back.

"How do we stop a demon?" Wren whispered sharply. "We are in way over our heads. We need to regroup, do some research, and not pick fights we can't finish."

"Good thing we're skilled stalkers," Shrike said.

Reluctantly, the siblings joined the group of people filing into the underground tunnel, rushing to catch the train before it started back toward the city. Shrike felt as if she was being watched every step of the way.

*\*\*\**

Shrike rechecked the address. Wren had outdone himself with the extensive list of all the occult shops and religious centers the city had to offer. She had been running them down all day and had nothing to show for it. Either demons were metaphors or extremely expensive to get rid of. A small bell by the door chimed as she entered the shop. She lingered in the doorway to kick the clumps of dirty snow off her boots and noted a thick line of salt that crossed the threshold.

"At least they're putting in the effort," she mumbled to herself.

The smells hit her all at once and she wrinkled her nose. These places always stank. Careful not to disrupt the line of salt, Shrike entered the store and glanced around. It had the same look and feel as all the other places she had visited today. Neatly packed shelves of trinkets and crystals. Jars of dried herbs, rows of books, and sealed tarot card decks.

The man behind the counter pretended to flip through his book as he watched her move around the displays. "Looking for anything in particular?"

"Yes, actually."

He looked her over. "Love potion?"

"No," Shrike said firmly.

"Good. I don't do that kind of stuff anyway. It's just creepy." He pulled a strip of red licorice from a nearby jar and bit off a chunk. "So you're looking to curse your boss, huh? Alright, I'm sure they deserve it."

"No," Shrike repeated. "I'm looking for information on demons."

The man slowed his chewing. "Demons?"

"Yes."

He laughed, "Hon, you do not want to play in their sandpit. Trust me."

"I have no intention of playing."

"Are you in trouble?"

"There's no point in going through the whole story if you don't know anything."

The man looked her over again. "What breed of demon are we

talking about?"

"Breed? There are different types?"

"Well, yeah."

"Can't you just give me general information?"

"Peacocks and penguins are both birds, but you lose some pretty important information trying to describe them both at the same time."

"That's true enough." Shrike chuckled softly, happy that Lark wasn't with her. She would never shut up about how the turn of phrase was a sign from their father. "So, how do you tell the difference?"

"Admittedly, it can be hard. They mostly tip their hands with how they operate." He finished off the last bit of licorice and wiped his hands off on his jeans. "But they do like to keep people guessing."

"Why is that?"

"It's a lot easier to get rid of them when you know exactly how to tailor your attacks."

"So, you can get rid of them?"

He nodded.

"I don't know what breed it is. It's trying to possess someone. Does that help narrow it down?"

"No, not at all. Most demons like their meat suits."

"Why is that?"

"Some can't physically manifest. Others are just extremely limited in what they can achieve."

"And what do they want to achieve, exactly?" Shrike asked.

"To be entertained." He shrugged.

"That's it?"

"What were you expecting? Birthing the antichrist? Maybe some of them are about that life but, generally, they don't work and play well with others. Even their own kind. They're sadists. They're only happy when they're making someone suffer. Can you tell me anything more?"

"I keep seeing a shadow."

"That could still be quite a few of them," he said.

Shrike thought for a moment. "This friend of mine. He came very close to having a deadly accident. He's fine now. He didn't get hurt. But it was a close call."

The man pulled another strip of licorice from the jar and chewed on it thoughtfully. "I know a few breeds that would be attracted to that kind of host. Tell ya what? Give me a few hours and I'll set up a basic exorcism kit."

"I heard you need a religious official to perform an exorcism. Is that true?"

"Nah, they just have more experience, that's all. I'll make sure that you get step by step instructions."

"And this will get rid of it?"

"This stuff happens a lot more than people give credit for." He looked at his watch. "You know what, come back tomorrow morning."

"How much will this cost?"

"Fifty all up. Plus tax. I want to help you, but I still have to make a living."

It was the best price she had been offered all day. "Alright. I'll pay on pickup."

"Cool. Oh, until this is all set, keep your friend in a circle of salt. It repels evil. And give him one of these." He ducked under the counter and retrieved a garland.

She hesitantly moved to take it. "Garlic? Really?"

"There's a reason it got into the folklore. Look, if I'm wrong, he stinks for a night. If I'm right, he stinks and doesn't get demonically possessed." He wiggled the garland, making the bulbs knock together. "Prevention is better than cure."

She took the garland. It was too big to put in her pocket, so she looped it around her neck, hiding it beneath her scarf. With a victorious smile, he folded the remains of the candy strip into his mouth.

"See you bright and early tomorrow."

Nodding, Shrike turned and headed for the door. Out of habit, she checked for security cameras, finding one posted above the door. She flipped her hood up and ducked her head. The crisp air pricked her skin as she left the warmth of the store behind. She set off back toward the subway station. This was the most progress that she had made, but she couldn't fully believe that it would work. There was still a part of her brain that refused to accept this new reality. She was still lost in thought when her phone began to buzz. Answering it on autopilot, she stumbled when she heard Barsotti huff.

"Finally, she answers."

"What are you doing?"

"I told you. I have a few questions."

Shrike clutched the phone. "This is harassment. Do I have to lodge a formal complaint against you?"

"I would love to see you come down to the station and do that."

"I haven't done anything illegal."

"That's debatable," Barsotti said. "I don't know why you're being so difficult."

"And I don't know why you're so fixated."

"Because I saw something," Barsotti blurted out.

"What?"

He heaved a strained sigh. "In the hospital. When I was prying Lisa off your neck. I saw…"

"What did you see?"

All the fight had gone from his voice when he whispered. "Something I can't explain. But my gut is telling me that you can."

"I don't know what you're talking about."

"You're a terrible liar."

Shrike pulled in a sharp breath. This was another complication they didn't have time for. "I'm heading into the subway—"

"Don't you dare hang up."

She ended the call and hit the speed dial for Wren as she entered the subway terminal.

\*\*\*

Wren used the last of his cold coffee to swallow another caffeine tablet. Their previous day with Trent hadn't proven anything. It felt like everything he had done since his father had died was utterly worthless. Days of poring over his laptop and he had nothing but a handful of stories and the weird twist in his gut that promised something bad was coming for them. He had decided to at least try and be ready. Not for his sake, but for his sisters. So, he had eaten a full meal, taken a shower, and tried to get a decent sleep. An endless string of nightmares had kept him up. And now, in the brightly lit public library, he couldn't remember a single one. All he remembered was the fear.

Rubbing his hands through his curls, he tossed another useless book on top of the pile. The impressive library sprawled out over two floors. Their occult section barely filled a shelf. He knew his sisters were relying on him. This was supposed to be what he was good at. But he was just spinning his wheels. His phone buzzed against the tabletop, and he tilted it just enough to read Lark's message.

"Trent's having another uneventful day," he whispered to himself. "Thank God for that."

With him doing research and Shrike running down leads, Lark had been left to tail the bus driver. It hadn't sat well with him. Shrike had reacted even worse. But their options were limited. They needed to keep an eye on him. It was a small comfort that he at least had a popular day shift. They could all meet up again before sundown. Wren checked the location against the map of the city, texted back a smiley face, and went back to work.

His hands hovered over the keyboard. "What am I missing?"

Wren flinched when his phone began to blare with an incoming call. Snatching it up quickly didn't prevent a few dirty looks from being thrown his way.

"Sorry," he whispered. "Family. You know how it is."

An elderly woman shushed him.

Wren answered the call. "Shrike?"

The woman shushed him again. He glared at her, wedged his phone between his shoulder and his ear, and hurriedly packed up his stuff.

"We have a problem," Shrike said.

"Are you okay?" Wren huffed when the woman loudly shushed him. "You see me packing up."

"What?" Shrike asked.

"Public libraries," he dismissed. Pulling his satchel strap onto his shoulder, he headed into the stacks. "What's the problem?"

"That cop saw something."

"Barsotti? What did he see?"

"I don't know."

Wren frowned. "How do you know he saw anything?"

"Because he told me! He keeps ringing, Wren! Gah! He's in my call waiting right now. He's fixated and he's got it into his head that we have answers."

"Shrike, you need to calm down."

"Are you out of your mind? Dad's dead, demons might be real, and I'm about to be stalked by a mentally unhinged man with a badge and a gun. We have to take him out first."

"No!" Wren glanced around. It didn't seem like his outburst had drawn attention, but he lowered his voice anyway. "Shrike, stay away from Barsotti."

"I'm not saying we kill him. I'm not insane. Just, maybe, break a leg. Something to get him on medical leave. Then—"

"Still breathing?"

Shrike's long, bitter sigh crackled through the phone.

"Still breathing," she said.

"How about thinking? Are you doing that?"

"I was just spit balling ideas," she grumbled.

"We'll discuss it tonight. You know Lark will want a say." A heavy thud made him turn. It was quiet enough to hear the hum of florescent lights. A single book now lay in the center of the empty row.

"Wren?" Shrike asked.

"What?" He asked.

"You stopped talking. Is everything alright?"

"I—" The words lodged in his throat when he heard the footsteps. Solid, heavy thuds stalking down the empty row.

"Wren?" Shrike snapped.

The footsteps stopped. He strained to hear anything other than his rapid, shallow breaths. Slowly, he backed away.

"Hey," Shrike said. "What's happening."

Another book was thrown from the shelf and Wren sprinted for the entrance.

"Call Lark. Meet me back at the hotel," he panted. "Now."

# Chapter 4

Lark's breath misted as it passed her chapped lips. Rubbing her hands together, she stretched her neck just enough to peer over the back of the seat before her. The cold didn't bother Trent as he pulled the bus into the next stop. People exhausted from their workday shuffled onboard. Each one complained about the cold, demanded he turn the heater up, and glared at him when he just shrugged. Trent kept his smile despite the growing resentment of the crowd, and Lark wondered if that was a sign he wasn't possessed. It was hard to imagine a demon being so cheerful. A shadow passed over her, and she stifled a yelp. A woman standing in the aisle heaved a sigh and gestured to Lark's feet.

"I'd like to sit down."

"Oh, sorry." Lark pressed her back against the side of the bus and drew her knees tightly against her chest.

"You could just put your feet down," the woman said.

"It's warmer like this."

Lark exaggerated her shiver and slightly widened her eyes, making herself look as vulnerable as possible. The woman scowled but eventually dumped herself into the free end of the bench seat. Lark still took it as a win. After a day of numbing cold and boredom, she was ready to relish anything resembling a victory. Peering over the seat again, she used the rearview mirror to glimpse Trent's face. He whistled a happy tune as he pulled the bus back onto the street. Suddenly, his reflected eyes flicked up to meet hers. Lark breathed on her gloved fingers to cover her face and sunk deeper into her hooded coat. Being able to hide within layers of clothing was the one upside of the bus being so insufferably cold.

They passed through an intersection, and Lark craned her neck to check the street names. Then she picked her phone up from her lap and typed out a quick text to Wren. The battery was struggling to keep a charge in the cold. The incoming call from Shrike almost killed it. She hurriedly answered.

"I was just about to text Wren," Lark said. "I was barely two minutes late—"

Shrike cut her off, "Plans have changed. Get to the hotel, now."

"What happened?"

"Wren—"

The phone call cut off. Lark cursed under her breath and looked at the dark screen. The battery was completely dead.

The woman sharing her seat tried to subtly avoid Lark's gaze.

"I'm sorry, I don't mean to bother you, but would you mind if I borrowed your phone?" Lark asked.

"I'd prefer not," the woman said.

"Oh, sure I understand." Lark fiddled with her phone and worried her bottom lip. "It's always that way, isn't it? The one time you leave your charger pack at home is the one time your mom…" She cut herself off and shook her head. "Sorry, I babble when I'm nervous."

The woman watched her for a moment out of the corner of her eye. "What happened to your mom?"

"The phone cut off before my sister could tell me. It's okay. It's not much longer to the hospital, right?"

The woman huffed and rummaged in her purse. They had gone a few more blocks before she pulled out her phone. Instead of handing it to Lark, she cursed under her breath, got to her feet, and hit the bus call button.

"This is my stop."

"But you just got on," Lark said.

"I've got three more transfers before I get home." The woman shoved her phone back in her purse and gave Lark a quick sympathetic smile. "Good luck with your mom."

She was moving to the doors before Lark could respond.

"Well, that sucks," Lark mumbled.

Unfurling a little bit, she peeked over the seats, scanning the crowd for someone else she could approach. All the people crowding around the exits blocked her view. She decided that it would act as enough of a cover and stretched out her aching legs. Sitting upright, she took a proper look around. They stopped and the doors opened with a hiss. Most of the crowd had filed out before she realized that she was the only passenger not moving. Tension gripped her chest. Lark stood up and darted for the exit. But between her heavy snow boots and her numb legs, she couldn't move quickly. She lumbered into the aisle and followed the last person to the back door. It snapped shut in her face and the bus lurched forward, throwing her off-balance. She staggered across the narrow aisle and dropped onto a seat. Bracing herself, she hurriedly looked around. The bus was empty. She was alone with Trent.

Lark grabbed for her phone before remembering that the battery was dead. Her eyes darted between Trent and the call button as the city flew past the windows. They were going too fast. Trent's soft whistle could barely be heard over the constant groan of the engine and the cracks of the changing gears. She eyed the button again but still hesitated to push it. Trent didn't seem to know she was there, and she didn't want to draw attention to herself.

Trent continued to whistle a simple nameless tune. Each note made her stomach twist. The sound grew louder as they weaved through the streets, picking up speed with every passing second. The short winter day was almost over, and deep shadows were settling over the snow-lined streets. Ice crystals formed in the edges of the windows, and her cheeks pricked with the cold. She leaned a little closer to the glass, the tension in her chest loosening as they approached the next stop. People gathered their belongings and moved closer to the curb. A few waved him down. Trent didn't stop. Lark could see their confusion and anger as the bus sped by. Lark glimpsed their angry faces before the bus turned into a narrow side street. There was barely enough room for the bus to pass by without sideswiping the parked cars. The engine strained. A few startled people jumped out of the way. Trent didn't stop whistling until he met her gaze in the rearview mirror.

"Your siblings aren't with you today," Trent said.

Lark's stomach dropped. He took another sharp turn that almost threw her from her seat. Outside, the streetlights flickered on.

"I knew I had seen you somewhere before." Trent watched her carefully. "It's those big eyes of yours. They have a way of sticking in a guy's memory."

"I'm pretty sure that you're mistaken," Lark said.

"I don't think so. It wasn't that long ago. My Christmas lights malfunctioned and set my tree on fire. My whole house almost went up. I would have died. But you and your family broke in and saved me."

She forced a smile. "Oh, right. Yeah, I remember now."

"Should I be offended that I'm so forgettable?" Trent laughed. "How many lives have you saved?"

The tone was light and playful, but Lark found something unsettling in his gaze. He was testing her reaction, watching to see if she would let anything slip.

"You're giving us way too much credit," Lark said sweetly. "The tree was only slightly on fire when we happened to pass by, hardly life-threatening at that point."

"Well, aren't you a positive little thing? Like a songbird in winter."

Forcing a shy smile, Lark snuck a glance out of the window. They passed through an intersection, and she couldn't recognize a single street name. Trent wasn't on the designated bus route anymore. She didn't know enough of the city to tell how far they had strayed or where they might be headed.

"Something wrong, little songbird?" Trent asked.

Lark met his gaze as the sun slipped beneath the horizon and darkness wrapped around them. His eyes reflected the glow of the console as he stared at her.

"No," Lark said. "Of course not."

Trent turned down an unlit service road. The cold air shifted behind her, and she locked herself in place, refusing to glance back. Images played out in her mind's eye. The darkness swelling and congealing, slowly coming together to forge a physical shape. A perfect silhouette of a man with a flat brimmed hat. Coldness spread across the back of her neck.

"Lark? Are you sure nothing's wrong?" Trent asked.

He sounded amused.

"I think I'm the next stop," Lark said. "My siblings will be waiting for me."

The bus sped up. The suspension squealed and the bus rocked as they exited the alley and entered a vast, open area of an abandoned parking lot. As she gripped the top of her chair, her mind whirled, trying to recall every moment of their previous interactions.

*Lark. He called me Lark. That can't be a guess, can it? Did we use our real names the night we saved him?* She couldn't remember. Wetting her suddenly too dry lips, Lark said, "I think you took a wrong turn."

"Nah, I'm just making up for lost time. The end-of-day rush always puts me a little behind."

A shiver went down her spine. "But we'll be back on the scheduled route soon, right?"

"Don't you worry, songbird. I know exactly where I'm taking you."

He started to whistle again. The next sharp turn caught Lark off guard and flung her back against the seats. A shadowy figure loomed over her. She jolted upright, astonished that the darkness itself couldn't pin her down. It had seemed solid enough but dispersed around her like smoke. Trent took another turn. His melody grew faster with each repetition. The tension in her chest tightened until she could barely breathe around it. Car horns blared as Trent weaved the bus through streets and back alleys.

She struggled to speak between her panted breaths. "Slow down. You'll hurt someone."

Trent ignored her. Random streetlights flashed against the

windows. With every burst, she expected to see the shadow man again. She never did. She only *felt* him there, one step behind her, inching ever closer to her spine.

"I want to get off," she blurted out.

"But your siblings are waiting for you."

"Stop the bus."

He didn't reply. The bus engine roared as it was pushed to its breaking point. Hot tears welled in her eyes as she clutched the seat.

"Please."

They shot out onto a street. Trent slammed on the breaks and yanked the wheel. Lark was tossed into the aisle. Her head cracked against the floor hard enough to leave white spots dancing in her vision. She winced and there was suddenly a hand before her. Lark flinched back with a squeal. Trent loomed over her, an amused grin on his face.

"How did you get up so fast?" she asked.

"Maybe you're just a little slow." He wiggled his fingers. "Take my hand."

She instinctively scrambled away and got to her feet. "No, thank you, I'm okay. I just need to leave."

His smile grew wider, and he stepped to the side, motioning with one hand to the front of the bus. The door was open. She looked over her shoulder and found the second exit still closed. The only way out was to slip through the narrow gap between him and the shadow-drenched seats.

"What are you waiting for?" Trent asked.

In her panic, all she could think was the single question her father had asked her a thousand times before: *Still breathing?* She placed a trembling hand against her chest, pushing hard against her snow coat to feel the fluttering of her heart.

"Still breathing," she mouthed.

"What was that?"

Clearing her throat, she forced a polite smile. "Thank you. I think I see my sister Excuse me."

Blood rushed through her ears, and her hands trembled. She didn't remember Trent being so tall, or broad, and her mind went wild with the thousand ways he could hurt her, possessed or not. Taking slow, deep breaths, she crept forward. His body heat felt like a furnace after so long in the bitter cold. Trent's eyes followed her every inch of the way. He kept one arm by his side, the other outstretched to the door. Even after she had squeezed past his body, he could still grab her. She felt forced into a game she didn't know the rules of. One wrong step and the illusion would break. Tears blurred her vision as she struggled to keep her pleasant smile.

The moment she stepped beyond the reach of his hand, she mumbled a "thank you" and threw herself out the door. Pain shot through her ankle as she landed awkwardly on the curb. She smothered a cry and staggered forward, putting some distance between her and the bus. She felt a presence close behind her and whipped around. The bus was already travelling down the long, empty stretch of familiar road.

"Oh, God. Please no." Swallowing thickly, she turned around and stared in horror at the neon lights of their motor inn. "It knows where we are."

\*\*\*

Shrike rubbed her aching neck and randomly flicked through the movie options. Switching hotels yet again hadn't settled either of her siblings. Wren was tearing himself apart trying to find the solutions to their problems, and Lark jumped at every shadow. It took sheer exhaustion to make them crash. The cheap room was too tiny for a cot. Shrike had let her siblings take the king-size bed and tried to arrange herself somewhat comfortably on the overstuffed armchair. It seemed like an impossible task. She rested her head against the wall and continued randomly switching through the channels. Warmth started to gather under her tracksuit. It felt like the first time she had been warm in days. It made it harder to keep her eyes open. Sitting up, Shrike rubbed her hand over her face. Her siblings had browbeat her into taking a small dose of her painkillers. That meant that she couldn't sleep. Not now anyway. Not until there was someone to keep watch. She couldn't take the dreams again.

Finding a replay of an old football game, she settled in to wait for dawn. All she had to do was hold out until one of her siblings woke up on their own. Then she could nap. Shrike eyed the line of salt that now marked their threshold before she decided to rest her eyes for just a moment. Hovering somewhere between awake and asleep, she could almost feel the shadows gathering beyond their door. An icy chill crept through the gaps around the window and drifted down to the carpet. She tried to open her eyes but couldn't. She could only sit there as the cold mist entered the room and crept toward her sleeping siblings.

A sharp buzz made her jerk upright. She gulped for air and hurriedly turned to the bed. Neither Wren nor Lark had stirred. The mist was gone. Or it had never really been there. Shrike looked around the quiet room, trying to sort reality from delusion. It unnerved her how hard it was becoming to tell the difference. Nothing felt real anymore. The only thing she could latch onto was that the game was still on. So if she had fallen asleep, she couldn't have been out for long. Her phone buzzed against her thigh again.

"Hello?" she groggily asked.

"Why didn't you inform me that you had moved hotels?" Barsotti demanded.

She straightened in her seat. After checking that neither of her siblings had been disturbed, she turned the volume down on the TV.

"Why are you looking for us, officer?"

"Either I've had a stroke, and no one has told me, or you have a real issue with hearing comprehension," Barsotti said.

"You are the most unprofessional cop I've ever met."

"And your opinion matters to me," Barsotti said. "Now, seriously, what happened?"

"Nothing."

"You are so bad at lying, it's actually insulting to hear you try," Barsotti said. "Hotel reception areas tend to have cameras. You guys looked spooked."

"You checked the footage?"

"You can't run from this thing, Shrike. Wherever you go, it's going to find you."

Shrike swallowed thickly, her eyes darting to the locked door and gaps between the thick curtains.

"How do you know that?"

"Because it only took me a few hours to find you," Barsotti said.

"What?"

"Look out your window. Come on, get up."

Shrike looked around the room. "You can see me?"

"No. It's three in the morning. I took an educated guess that you'd be lying down. I can see your window though. And if you open your curtains, you'll see me. Hurry up. It's cold out here." When Shrike hesitated, he added, "I'm accommodating, not patient. I've got no problem coming to your room, waking up your siblings, asking them a few questions. Or I could take you all down to the station if you'd feel more comfortable there."

"Stay where you are," Shrike said. "I'm getting up."

Crossing the small room, she kept her phone pressed to her ear and pulled back one side of the curtain, careful not to expose her siblings. A small parking lot and a strip of grass separated their hotel from a main road. The street was quiet but never deserted, and the surrounding stores catered to the all-night clientele. Shrike scanned the area and the few people that passed.

"Where are you hiding?" Shrike asked.

"Out of curiosity, how do you know I'm not one of the people walking by? Distance and winter gear makes it hard to tell."

"None of them have your cocky swagger."

"Oh? You remember how I walk? I'm flattered."

Shrike pulled the curtain back a little more. None of the cars were parked at an angle that would give a comfortable vantage point. But there was a diner across the street that would work well. The grocery store a bit further down had a display that would make a good blind. Although, from that far, he'd need binoculars to make out any details.

"It's a force of habit, officer. I part-time as a nature guide."

"You stalk for a living."

His thoughtful tone was as obnoxious as his smile and made her realize how much she was giving away. Her attention went to the bus stop in front of the hotel. Three frosted glass walls offered little shelter from the elements. It was brightly lit. Someone was leaning against the edge of the frame nearest the road, positioned so that their shadow wouldn't be cast over the back glass. From there, all the person had to do was peek around the edge and they'd have a straight line of sight to Shrike's hotel room window.

Before she could expose his hiding place, he waved, his shadow swaying over the surrounding grass. "See me now?"

"Yes. I'll be down in a second."

"Are you sure? It'll be warmer up there."

"The diner is open."

"Great, you can buy me a coffee," Barsotti said lightly.

Shrike hung up and begrudgingly pulled on her coat and boots. She used the hotel's stationary to leave her siblings a note, grabbed a room key, and slipped out into the cold. Barsotti remained in the shelter as she hurried down the exterior staircase. It was a still night that made the air feel heavy. Pulling her jacket closer, she darted across the parking lot, keeping her eyes on the bus stop. Barsotti inched further into the shelter, his shadow becoming a dark shape on the back glass. His solid silhouette leaned against something and crossed its arms. He had stood the same way in the hospital, and it annoyed her just as much now as it did then. Shrike stepped onto the grass and froze. His silhouette was *exactly* the same as it had been in the hospital. Lean and smooth. There was no hint of a bulky winter jacket or bundled scarf or anything that could protect him from the freezing night air. He didn't shiver or huddle for warmth. Barsotti's shadow leaned against nothing and watched her. Shrike trailed her eyes down the shape. The glass ended a few feet above the concrete floor. She couldn't see his shoes. Her heart quickened its pace as she crouched to get a better look. No one was in the shelter. There was only the shadow.

Shrike's breath caught in her throat. The shadow heard her. She felt its amusement as it unfurled itself. Its limbs elongated and grew sharp. The darkness gathered against the glass and dripped down to pool over the concrete slab. Shrike screamed. She spun and bolted back toward the hotel, feeling the shadow closing in from behind.

# Chapter 5

Wren jerked upright. Sleep fogged his mind and muddled his movements. Beside him, Lark scrambled onto her feet, tripping a little when the blankets tangled around her legs.

"Shrike?" Blinking owlishly, Lark turned to Wren. "You heard her too, right?"

He nodded and grabbed his long jacket off the end of the bed, tugging it on over his pajamas.

"Shrike?" Lark called.

The hotel room was too small for her to be hiding anywhere. If she didn't call out from the bathroom, she wasn't here. Zipping up his coat, Wren grabbed his glasses off the bedside table, reading the note Shrike had left.

"Barsotti's here," he said. "Bus stop out front."

"She wouldn't scream because of him," Lark said, already yanking on her boots.

Wren fought to keep her panic from affecting him. "He might be arresting her."

"Or it's the demon. I told you, Trent wasn't right when I—" Lark pulled the curtains back and gasped.

Shrike was sprinting across the parking lot, weaving between the cars in a mad dash to get back to the hotel.

"Wren?" Lark whimpered. "Something's really wrong."

"Stay here." Wren jumped into his boots and stumbled out of the door. "Lock the—"

Lark shoved past him and sprinted for the stairs. "Shrike! What's going on?"

Her foot struck a patch of ice. She slipped and toppled down the staircase.

"Lark!" Wren shook off the last haze of sleep and sprinted to the railing. His little sister had stopped about halfway down the length of concrete steps. She was curling up in pain, one hand nursing her head. "Lark? Are you okay?"

Lark winced.

"Get inside!" Shrike screamed as she neared the base of the stairs. "Go! Run!"

Lark's eyes widened as she struggled to get up. Wren darted forward. By the time he looked up again, the shadows around him had changed. There was a slick luster to them and a solidness they couldn't possibly have. They congealed together and fell to the balcony in thick mucus-like globs. They splattered across his feet, each tiny droplet cold enough to burn. The darkness gripped the soles of his boots like tar. Grabbing the railing with both hands, he dragged himself forward. The substance bubbled and oozed around his feet. His legs ached from fighting against its pull. Sweat dripped down his face despite the cold. The mucus shadows welled until he was almost dragged down to his ankles.

A nearby room door swung open and a shaft of light washed over him. In an instant, the darkness returned to harmless shadows. The tension that had held him in place suddenly released, and he dropped to the floor.

"What the hell are you doing?" a man snapped, standing in his doorway. "Do you know what time it is?"

"Was that real?" Wren whimpered. He smacked the shadows nearest him. None of them were tacky. None of them had any substance at all. "But... but I felt it. I did."

For the first time, he couldn't trust the evidence before him. He looked up to the stranger that was still in the doorway.

"Am I going insane?"

The man blinked at him. "Yeah, I just wanted to sleep. Keep it down."

He shut the door and snuffed out the light, leaving Wren to the gathering shadows.

*\*\**

Lark's head throbbed. She had managed to catch herself halfway down the stairs, but her whole body still hurt from the fall. A chilling mist pushed through the gaps between the steps. Blinking to clear her vision, she looked around, needing to catch sight of her siblings. Shrike and Wren were both approaching her, each one ordering her in a different direction. All she could think was to get to her feet. Rolling onto all fours, she bit back a yelp and glimpsed the darkness below the staircase. A hand struck out of the shadows and latched onto her wrist. The flesh was pure ice. She pulled back but couldn't break free. Trent's face emerged like a moon from behind clouds, pale and gleaming. His eyes rolled back in his head until the only color came from his popping blood vessels. His jaw hung limp, his swollen tongue making him choke and gasp.

"Found you," he rasped.

His hand tightened around her wrist. She screamed and threw herself back. The fingers released her, and she toppled down the rest of the stairs. Blood splashed over her tongue. Pain whited out her vision and, with one last solid thud, she hit the base of the stairs. Shrike was on her before her thoughts could clear. Strong hands pressed over Lark's body, testing to see the extent of the damage. Everything hurt but nothing was broken.

"Come on. We need to get back to the room." Shrike tried to be gentle, but it seemed impossible to move Lark without some pain.

"No! Trent's hiding under there. Didn't you see him?" Lark gasped.

Wren barreled down the stairs and shoved his sisters, forcing them to move.

"Go, go, go," he said.

Wren grabbed Lark's arm, pulled it over his shoulders, and half dragged her into the parking lot.

"Something is out there," Shrike argued.

"Something is up there!" Wren babbled. "We need light. And people. One of them scared it off and I'm not sure which."

Lark clenched her teeth to keep from whimpering. Everything hurt and leaning on Wren was slowing them both down. They hobbled a few steps before Shrike intervened. She easily bundled Lark into her arms, cradling her against her chest as she took off at a sprint.

"We can't go near the bus stop," Shrike said.

Wren led them to the nearest streetlamp. It flickered and buzzed as they approached and died the moment they entered its ring of light. Shadows swirled around them.

Lark pointed across the street. "The grocery store."

Neither of her siblings hesitated. Wren pressed close, fearful of every shadow, while Shrike kept looking to the illuminated bus stop. Lark followed her gaze and screamed. A gaunt, distorted creature hunched against the glass. It was too big to fit into the shelter. As they ran, it unfolded itself, creeping out of its hiding place. It was an inky black mass that bled seamlessly into the shadows. Lark lost sight of the creature, but she still felt it following them. Every streetlight they passed died.

Shrike tightened her grip on Lark and ran onto the road, Wren a step behind. A car screeched to a stop. Lark barely noticed it. Her attention was locked on the creature that seemed to flicker in and out of existence. She strained but couldn't get a decent look at it. It was always just out of sight. They jumped up onto the sidewalk. The corner store lights strobed as they neared the entrance. Each burst of darkness allowed the grotesque creature to lunge forward. It was right behind them as Shrike crossed the threshold. Lark watched helplessly as the pitch-black mass surged forward. Shrike screamed. The back of her jacket ripped open, spewing out small white feathers tipped with blood. Shrike staggered and fell. She tossed Lark aside an instant before crashing into a fresh produce display. The wood siding cracked under her weight. Shrike hit the ground in an avalanche of onions and garlic bulbs. The lights flickered once more before stabilizing.

"Where is it?" Wren panted. "It was right there. It was right behind us."

Shrike hissed between her clenched teeth and gripped her shoulder. Blood seeped between her fingers.

"Shrike?" Lark gasped.

The siblings converged on Shrike and gently forced her hand away.

"This is a bite mark," Wren said as he peered through the hole in her jacket. "Shadow demons can bite? But how? It's not tangible. It's not possible. None of this is possible."

"Wren, stop." Lark dropped her voice to a whisper as the few people in the store rushed over. "I saw Trent. Something is wrong with him. I think that thing came with him."

"It called me," Shrike winced. "It sounded exactly like Barsotti. It intentionally lured me out of the room. It's smart."

The people around them spotted the blood and their anger turned to concern and confusion.

"What do we do now?" Lark whispered in a rush. "It found us again. We can't run."

"We fight," Shrike said.

In their last moment of privacy, Wren mouthed the word "exorcism". His sisters nodded.

Sucking in a deep breath, Lark whirled on the coming people, already trying to form the right lies for the barrage of questions thrown her way. They needed to patch up Shrike. Everything else could wait.

\*\*\*

Shrike's back ached and her brain was exhausted after teetering on the edge of chaos for so long. Lark had kept most of the crowd away from her. Having something to do, a way to occupy her mind, had allowed her little sister to hold herself together. Shrike hadn't paid much attention to the stories Lark had spun for the people that had demanded an explanation. Wren had fixated on the bite mark like solving that riddle would fix everything. When no one was looking, he had hurriedly whispered snippets of information into Shrike's ear. The wound had bled for a while, even though it wasn't too deep. He was sure it was a bite mark. Each tooth had cleanly punctured the flesh and left her feeling cold, like tiny slivers of ice were trapped under her skin. The chill didn't ease the ache.

They lingered in the store until dawn. Then Shrike ran back to the hotel to get their wallets and paid the bill. By then, Lark had struck up a friendship with the employees. It got them out of paying for the damaged display. They promised to make something up for their boss. Shrike had wanted to take a taxi to the occult shop, but they couldn't afford the trip. It was looking likely that they would need every cent to get out of the city when the time came.

Shrike rolled her injured shoulder as they trudged up the steps that connected the subway platform to the street. Clouds sat heavy over the sky, keeping the morning light murky and dull. People rushed around them, either heading to work or coming home. Shrike didn't like it. She had never done well with crowds. Being surrounded by strangers put her on edge and it was only worse now. She couldn't stop eyeing every face with suspicion. A demon could be squatting in any one of them and there'd be no way to know until it was too late. They reached the top of the staircase, and Lark paused to rub her hip.

"Are you okay?" Shrike asked.

"Just a little sore," Lark answered. "Which way is the store?"

"Bullshi—" Shrike doubled over with a grunt when Wren nudged her sharply in the ribs. She glared at him and motioned before them. "Two blocks that way."

The siblings huddled close together as they worked their way through the growing crowd. They rounded the bend and then stopped short. The front of the occult store was blocked off by strategically parked police cruisers and a string of yellow tape. A spotless white coroner's van passed by the shocked siblings. They retreated around the edge of the building, hiding there to survey the crime scene.

"Maybe it's not related," Lark said. "It could just be a robbery gone wrong. A normal everyday event. Nothing to do with demons at all."

"It followed me," Shrike said.

"This is the man who said he could help us?" Wren asked.

Bile burned the back of Shrike's throat. "Yes."

"We don't know he's the victim," Lark insisted.

"Stop it, Lark. I brought the demon here and it killed him. We all know it."

Lark threw a sympathetic look at her sister. "We don't know."

"It's not your fault," Wren said. "I told you to come here. His death is on me."

"It's all of us or none of us," Lark said. "That's the way it's always been and it's not changing now. And really, it doesn't matter at this point, does it? We've got to take care of Trent before this happens again." Her eyes darted between her siblings. "So, what do we do now?"

Shrike's stomach churned and her head pounded. Rubbing her forehead, she tried to think. "I was supposed to pick up the kit this morning. It was going to include step-by-step instructions."

"So he might have prepared it already," Lark said. "That's good. It's probably in there, right? We just need to go and get it. You didn't tell him your real name, did you?"

"No. And I have no idea what it would look like or include."

"I'm sure it's labeled. You'll know it when you see it," Lark assured.

"I can't go in and get it. Even if I make it inside, the shelves are too low, too widely spaced. Someone will spot me for sure."

Lark and Wren shared a look.

"I'll go," Lark said. She held up a hand when Wren started to protest. "I'm the smallest."

"There's a back office. There's probably a window or door you'll be able to use," Shrike said.

"She'll need a distraction. Something that will draw everyone out front but won't really have any lasting consequences." Wren winced and caught Shrike's gaze. "You up for a fight?"

"Are you sure they won't charge you with something? I mean, you're disturbing the peace," Lark said.

"They have a murder to worry about," Wren replied.

"We'll give you five minutes to work your way around." Shrike glared at Wren. "I'm throwing the first punch. Just in case the police do care."

Wren groaned. "Be gentle."

The siblings used their phones to find a nearby diner that could serve as their meeting point. Then Lark slipped away. Wren shifted his weight as they counted down. When the time came, they inched around the corner. Keeping close to the wall to avoid attention too early, they moved directly opposite the crime scene. There were a few officers moving around but none of them really looked in their direction.

"You ready?" Shrike asked.

Wren sighed. "For the sake of my ego, let me get at least one punch in."

She swung before she could think better of it. Keeping her fist loose softened the blow but there was still enough force behind it to make Wren stagger to the side. He glared at her, fixed his glasses, and ran at her with a yell. He ducked to drive his shoulder into her stomach. Fighting her impulse to pound her fists against his exposed back, Shrike took the blow. It knocked the air from her lungs and drove her back a few steps. People had noticed. Unfortunately, the civilians were the first to move toward them.

"Sorry," Shrike whispered.

Doubling over her brother, she wrapped her arms around his waist. He was a slight man. She could lift him easily and throw him with relatively little strain. The motion tore at her wounds. Pain wracked her body and forced her to stagger. She threw him harder than she meant to. He yelped as he toppled over the road. Getting onto his knees, Wren pushed back his curls and glared at her. She cringed but didn't apologize. There were too many eyes on them now. Wren pushed past a stranger that was trying to get between them and charged toward her again. She let him get his hit this time. Her head snapped to the side and pain sliced along her jaw and down her neck.

"Knock it off!" a voice bellowed before they were shoved apart.

Shrike's stomach dropped as Barsotti stepped between them.

"You have to be kidding me." Barsotti jabbed a finger at each sibling, growled at them to stay put, and glanced over his shoulder. "I've got it."

The officers that had been running over hesitated. Barsotti had to reassure them again before they returned to the crime scene.

"Against the wall," Barsotti ordered. "Both of you."

Shrike glanced to her brother. He nodded encouragingly for her to obey and led the way back to the sidewalk. Shrike hadn't even noticed the cars waiting for them to get off the road.

"What the hell are you two up to?" Barsotti demanded.

Shrike's insides squirmed like a pit of snakes. She hadn't imagined it. The demon had perfectly mimicked his voice. *If it can sound like him, who else could it sound like?* The thought left her cold. Barsotti scowled and clicked his fingers an inch from her nose.

"That wasn't rhetorical. What are you doing, Shrike?"

She flinched back from his fingers. "Nothing."

"It was a private dispute," Wren cut in. "We apologize—"

"She was clearly pulling her punches." Barsotti gestured to his still-healing eye. "I've got enough experience with her temper to know when she's faking it."

"He's my brother. Of course, I'd be gentle with him."

Barsotti wasn't listening. He frowned as he carefully scanned the street.

"Where's the little one?"

"What?" Shrike asked.

"Your sister," Barsotti snapped. He paused and locked her with a piercing gaze. "Did you have something to do with what happened here?"

"What happened?" Wren asked.

Barsotti waved him off. "Nope. She answers."

"Why me?"

"Because you're easy to read," Barsotti said. He jabbed a thumb over his shoulder. "If I check that security footage, am I going to find one of you on it?"

"Lark is picking up our father's remains," Wren cut in.

"Now, why wouldn't you tell me that?"

Shrike couldn't answer. Wren used the opening to slip a little closer to Barsotti, subtly pushing him back from Shrike and dropping his voice to a whisper.

"Shrike was practically our father's shadow and she's really struggling with his… absence. She's been a little erratic. I'm sorry, I know our behavior was inappropriate."

Barsotti kept his slight smile even as his gaze sharpened. "And why are you here?"

"I'm sorry?"

"Why aren't you getting the remains with Lark?" Barsotti demanded. "Collecting your father's ashes seems like a pretty emotional event. One you'd do as a family. But here you two are, squabbling in front of my murder scene instead of being with your sister. That seems odd to me."

Wren cleared his throat. "We're all dealing with our grief in our own way."

"I'm not buying it." Barsotti turned to Shrike, his gaze as sharp as an ice pick. "Where's your sister?"

She tried to think but couldn't come up with anything more than half truths. "I'm not sure of her exact location."

"That's not a good enough answer," Barsotti pressed.

Anger was a familiar grounding sensation and she clung to it now. "I don't have to give you an answer."

"Oh, I think you do. Bad things just keep happening around you guys."

"Then go get the officer that's actually in charge and I'll talk to them." Shrike balled her fists and lifted her chin. Blood wept from her wounds and chilled against her skin. "Because you're not the one in charge of anything, right?"

"You love pointing that out."

"And you love pretending you have more authority than you do," Shrike countered. There was movement over Barsotti's shoulder. She glanced up to see Wren tapping his phone. Lark had been a lot quicker than anticipated. "We're going to leave now."

"Nah, I don't think so," Barsotti said.

"What?"

"Yeah, I'm taking you up on your offer. I'm going to get the guy in charge." He motioned another uniformed officer over and smiled at the Rose siblings. "You guys get nice and comfortable. This might take a while."

# Chapter 6

Wren rummaged through the 'kit' as they hurried down the sidewalk. There wasn't much to it. A short list of instructions, a tin of salt that Lark now fiddled with, and a small vial of clear liquid. He pulled the vial out again, holding it up to the fading sunlight to better see the flecks that had gathered in the bottom. The multiple colors suggested that there were a few different ingredients. But they were all too ground up for him to even guess what they were. The store owner hadn't written the recipe down.

"I would have preferred to do this with some sunlight," Lark said.

"We can wait until dawn," Shrike said, nervously eyeing the houses around them.

Interior lights cast shadows over the drawn curtains.

"We can't just leave it alone to do what it wants for the night," Lark insisted. "It could hurt someone. We have to end this now."

"It doesn't seem smart to do this at night," Shrike insisted.

"We've seen the shadow demon during the day," Wren said. "The fact that it's bolder at night doesn't necessarily mean it's stronger during those hours. And at least this way, we'll have some cover."

"I still don't like it," Shrike muttered.

"Well, winter days are short, and you guys took forever," Lark said.

"That wasn't our fault," Shrike said.

Wren pushed his glasses up his nose. "Well, it was kind of your fault."

"How?" Shrike demanded. "They had no right to hold us."

"Exactly. All you had to do was keep your mouth shut and we would have been out of there in an hour. But, no. Every time we were just about to leave, you'd get into another pissing match with Barsotti and give him just enough to hold us until he 'checked something out'." He tucked the bag under his arm to do the appropriate air quotes.

"It's like he was doing it on purpose."

"He was, Shrike," Wren huffed. The last of the daylight died, and darkness took hold. "This is why Dad always tells you to let us do the talking. Because you are the most easily manipulated person on the planet."

"Guys," Lark cut in.

They turned to her, and she motioned with her chin down the quiet suburban street. Trent's house was just ahead. Wren felt the shift as they settled into their well-honed roles. Habit drove their hastily forged plan, and he hoped that it would be enough. His stomach churned as he followed his sisters into the shadows between the houses. They knew the layout from the previous stalking sessions and, in a small twist of luck, none of the neighbors had gotten new pets or set up security lights. They moved as shadows from one yard to the next, drawing closer to Trent's house.

Wren fought against all the thoughts crawling through his mind. The last time he had been here, the darkness had made him feel safe. There was a certain power to it. A sense of control in knowing that he would only be seen when he chose to reveal himself. Now he felt like the darkness had eyes. The hair on the back of his neck rose and, with every step, it became harder to breathe. They jumped over the last fence and dropped into Trent's backyard. A single unstable light escaped the dark interior of the house. Everything was quiet.

The siblings paused in a final silent check with one another. Lark held up the box of salt. Shrike unzipped the top of her jacket just enough to expose the thick cord of rope she was carrying. Wren pulled the fishing line from his pocket.

"You're sure you can pronounce the words correctly?" Shrike whispered. "I'm not even sure that's a language."

"The store owner wrote it phonetically," Wren replied.

"You have to repeat it three times, right?" Lark asked.

"Yes."

Shrike nodded, placed a hand against her chest, and took a slow breath. Wren felt compelled to mirror the motion, feeling his pulse beat rapidly against his fingertips. They shared one last glance before Shrike led the way to the kitchen window. Their father had rigged it months ago to ensure that they would have a point of entry when the time came to intervene. Trent could have noticed and replace the broken latch. Wren held his breath as Shrike carefully inched the window open. It rattled against its frame. Shrike gave it a hard shove. With a soft crunch of frost, the window slid open. They paused. No lights flicked on. No alarms blared. Trent had the day off. They hadn't been able to track him today, given Barsotti's interference. If he wasn't home now, he would be soon. But the house remained silent and dark.

Waiting a heartbeat longer, Shrike slipped through the window. Wren lingered until she motioned for them to follow then pulled himself through the gap and onto the kitchen counter. The house was deathly cold. The doorway to the living room was across from him. Light flickered through the threshold, making shadows dance across the walls. Shrike crept silently over the tiles and peeked into the living room. She waved to him, and he motioned for Lark to enter. His fingers had grown numb before all three of them were inside. Dad had always insisted that they never go anywhere without an exit strategy, and Lark's encounter at the bus had reminded them to take his advice. They left the window open and gathered in the living room.

The glow of the streetlights illuminated the drawn curtains. A fire crackled in the hearth, but it offered little warmth. Wren's brow furrowed as he tiptoed further into the room. The room looked like he remembered. The half-burned Christmas tree had been left to rot in the corner, still dressed in the charred baubles. He hadn't even cleaned up the fire extinguisher foam, leaving it to dry and flake.

*He never cleaned up,* Wren thought. *How long did the demon wait before taking him?*

A soft creak snapped him out of his thoughts. His breath caught in his throat as he looked to the front door. It took another sound for him to realize the noises were coming from inside the house. He turned to the pitch-black hallway that led to the bedrooms. Nothing stirred.

The siblings rushed to organize themselves. Lark retrieved a kitchen chair and set it in the center of the room. Shrike and Wren positioned themselves on either side of the hallway opening and crouched down. Wren looped the fishing line around his gloved hand a few times before checking the hallway. It was still empty. He tossed the remaining tangle of fishing line over to Shrike, who quickly looped it around her own hand. They pulled taut to test their makeshift trip-line before placing their hands on the floor. The unstable firelight helped it blend into the shadows. Once they were ready, they nodded to Lark. Taking in a steadying breath, she gripped the back of the chair and gently rattled it, shifting it back and forth as she shuffled her feet. The series of soft noises sounded like she was trying her best to be stealthy but failing. Lark had perfected the art of being bait.

It didn't take long to get Trent's interest. Muffled footsteps shuffled down the hallway. Wren's hands shook. His heartbeat quickened. The sound drew closer. Lark gasped and ducked down behind the chair, cowering. She looked like she had been caught off guard trying to set something up. A small, helpless little thing mistakenly thinking she was hidden. Trent emerged from the shadows. His veins stood stark against his pale flesh. His body jerked and twitched, and he dragged his left foot like he couldn't quite lift it. Wren tightened his grip on the cord. Trent stilled just before entering their trap. Across from him, Shrike bared her teeth with barely contained rage. Her broad shoulders tensed but she kept still and quiet.

"I see you," Trent sang. Lark gasped, and a taunting smile curled his lips. "What are you up to?"

Lark peered up at him. "Nothing."

"Nothing?"

"I just wanted to check on you."

"How sweet." Trent's voice distorted, and the shadows darkened.

"I'm not new to this, child."

Trent surged into the room. He didn't go for Lark. He went straight for Shrike. Wren threw himself back and the cord pulled taut. Trent stumbled but kept going. With a cry, Shrike threw herself up and drove her shoulder into Trent's gut. The blow made the man topple. Wren scrambled forward and grabbed the man's wrists but didn't have the strength to pin him down. Trent surged up but Shrike was on him in a second. She looped the fishing line around Trent's neck and pulled until the man gagged and gasped.

"Don't kill him," Wren said.

"Start the chant," Shrike ordered and wrangled the choking man onto his knees.

She positioned herself behind Trent, using her height and strength to keep him off-balance. Wren poured the contents of the vial over Trent's head then started the chant. He barely got through three words before his mind went blank.

"Damn it." He fumbled with the paper.

The room darkened until he couldn't make out the words. He ran toward the fire while Shrike wrestled with Trent. Lark held the chair steady until Shrike shoved Trent down into it. Wren started the chant while Lark circled the chair, pouring out a line of salt.

"The ring of salt is done." She clutched the box to her chest and retreated to Wren's side. "The demon should be contained."

Wren tipped the sheet to the light to read the last few lines. Trent began to screech. His skin bulged and blood dripped from his eyes. Shrike strained to keep him in the chair.

"Lark, I can't get the rope," she snapped.

"Keep reading," Lark ordered before darting forward.

Wren's eyes flicked between the paper and his sisters as he read. Lark pulled the rope out from Shrike's jacket to secure Trent to the chair. The instant the knots were in place, Shrike looped her arm around Trent's neck and squeezed. Wren kept reading.

"We can gag him," Lark said.

"Get away," Shrike ordered.

Wren trembled as he repeated the chant. Lark jumped over the ring of salt and rejoined him. The Christmas tree toppled over as the floor began to tremble. The window rattled and the fire flared. Trent strained against Shrike and the rope, his legs shaking and eyes bulging. Wren finished the last repetition and it all stopped. Trent fell limply against the chair. Panting, Shrike looked to her siblings before slowly releasing her grip.

"Is that it?" Lark asked.

"That's the last of the instructions," Wren said.

"Did it work, Shrike? Do you think it worked?"

Shrike leaned in to the man to check his face. In a sudden burst, Trent threw his arms out, easily snapping the rope and surging to his feet. He backhanded Shrike; the single blow sending her across the room.

"Shrike!" Lark squealed.

Coughing up blood, Shrike rolled up onto her knees. The fire sputtered and dwindled into embers. The cold rushed in to cover the walls with a thick layer of frost. Trent chuckled.

"That's it?" His voice distorted into a growl. "It's been so long. I had hoped you'd put up a bit more of a fight. An evening of entertainment at least."

Trent toed the line of salt and smiled.

"Why didn't it work?" Lark whispered to Wren. "It should have worked."

"It was a lie." Trent snickered, his flesh rippling over his bones. He nudged the line. "I'm no ghost, child. I am so much more."

The last of the embers was snuffed out. An instant before the light died, Wren saw the possessed man step out of the ring.

"Run!" Shrike screamed.

Wren grabbed Lark and sprinted for the kitchen door. The dark winter night had already settled in, leaving only a pale light to flood in through the open kitchen window. Darkness rippled over the walls and the floor shook. He didn't dare look back as he helped Lark scramble up onto the counter. The window slammed shut before her. She pulled but it wouldn't open. Dark taunting laughter rolled around the walls. Wren pressed against the counter and twisted around, trying to catch sight of Trent. The man sprinted from the shadows. Wren braced himself but, before the possessed man could touch him, Shrike jumped on Trent's back and knocked him off-balance. They fell into the kitchen table, the wood snapping under their bodies.

"Go!" Shrike commanded.

Wren bolted for the back door. He fumbled blindly with the lock and handle but couldn't work them open. Shrike's agonized cries made him panic. Illuminated by the moonlight, Lark grabbed the toaster and smashed the window.

"Come on!" Lark cried.

Wren jumped up onto the counter. "Go," he ordered Lark before turning back to the darkness. He could see the movement of bodies but couldn't tell them apart. "Shrike?"

"Get Lark out of here!"

He hesitated before leaping through the broken window. The moonlight was almost blinding after the deep shadows. Lights flicked on in the neighboring houses.

"Someone's going to call the cops," Lark panted. "We have to help Shrike. We have to go."

The house fell silent. The neighbors' exterior light flicked on. The siblings ducked closer to the dividing gate to keep out of sight.

"Trent?" a stranger called. "Is everything all right?"

A scream pierced the night and made them jump. Shrike hurled herself through the broken window. Flopping onto the grass, she writhed in pain and screamed again.

"Trent?!" the neighbor cried out. "I'm getting help!"

More lights flicked on, eating away the sibling's hiding places. Shrike sobbed and rolled up onto all fours. She crawled for her siblings as Wren and Lark ran to join her. It took both of them to get the huge woman on her feet. Going over the fence wasn't an option in her condition, so they darted down the side of the house.

"I see you!" the neighbor said.

"She's calling—"

"We know, Lark," Wren panted.

He cringed away from every window they passed, but Trent didn't emerge. They burst out of the darkness and staggered onto the front lawn. The glow of the streetlights was comforting and terrifying at once. They didn't know where they were going. They just ran from the house and Trent's low laugh.

* * *

Shrike squeezed her eyes shut and pressed her forehead against her knees. Her body trembled, each tremor bringing a new wave of crushing pain. She pulled her hood tightly over her head and held her breath. Wren had an arm wrapped around her shoulders. He was pressed close enough that he would feel it if she cried.

"It's okay," Wren whispered. "Lark will get Dad's ashes, and we'll get the hell out of here."

Shrike's phone buzzed. Wren rejected the call with a grunt.

"Barsotti?" Shrike mumbled.

"He won't stop calling."

Lark was in the next room, using her charms to get the workers to hurry up, but she seemed so far away. None of them felt comfortable turning off their phones and severing that point of contact.

"We'll be out of the city before he can track us down," Wren insisted. "It doesn't matter that the neighbors saw us. It was so dark. And there was a fence. They won't be able to give a proper description."

"It was enough for Barsotti," Shrike whispered.

"We don't know that. He might just be calling about this morning." Wren said. "How would he even hear about it? Is he monitoring every reported crime?"

"Maybe."

"No, I can't believe that. I don't think Trent will get the police involved anyway. Why would a demon want the attention? The more people that know about them, the more likely it is that someone would find a way to hurt them. They're stronger in the shadows." Wren's rambling was cut short.

Shrike lifted her head. Another family had entered the crematorium. There were still a few hours before it closed and there seemed to be a steady stream of people coming to collect their dead. The family gave them a polite nod of acknowledgment and a few sympathetic smiles. The siblings could tell the exact moment they noticed the blood and bruises Shrike's hood couldn't hide. She looked away.

Wren dipped his head to whisper in her ear, "What did Trent do to you?"

"Nothing. A few bites. That's all," she said.

"Shrike—"

"I'm just not used to feeling helpless," she admitted. "He made sure I knew that it was all a game to him. That I was so powerless it didn't matter if I lived or died. I'm nothing."

Not knowing what to say, Wren pulled her into a tight hug. She sunk into the comforting touch despite the pain. They only parted when the doors opened again. Lark rushed into the room, a small brown box clutched to her chest.

"I've got him," Lark whispered as she ran a fingertip along the edges.

Shrike couldn't stop the wail that escaped her. She crumbled in on herself, desperately gasping for air in between heavy broken sobs. Lark rushed over and dropped next to her siblings. They clung to each other, the box of ashes carefully cradling between them.

"I should have been in there for the cremation," Shrike said.

"None of us were there," Wren soothed.

"Exactly," Shrike said. "He shouldn't have gone through that alone."

"Dad didn't want us to see that stuff," Lark said. "He was very clear about that, remember? He didn't want that to be our last memory of him. No viewing the cremation. No big funeral service."

"I'd rather have memories of the fire than that hotel room." Shrike clutched the box, her vision blurring with tears. "Do you think he called for me? When Lisa was hurting him, do you think he called for me?"

"No." Wren grabbed her chin and forced her to meet his gaze. "Dad wouldn't have called for any of us because he would never risk drawing us into that kind of danger. His life's work was all about keeping people safe."

Shrike sobbed. "His life's work was a lie, Wren. How many people do you think will die *because* of what we did? Dad would be so ashamed."

In the silence that followed, they remembered the other family. Shrike angrily wiped the tears from her eyes. The strangers had kept a respectful distance, making it unlikely that they had overheard anything, but she couldn't stop herself from glaring at them.

"We should go," Lark whimpered.

"No, we shouldn't," Wren said abruptly, his eyes locked on the mourning family. "Shrike's right. Dad would be ashamed. He gave up so much to help these people. He would never leave Trent to end up like Lisa. He'd never just walk away when he knew people would die. We have to stop this."

"We tried," Lark said. "Shrike almost died."

"I know," Wren said.

"Well, unless you suddenly know how to stop a demon, I vote we get the hell out of here."

Shrike frowned. "We do know how."

"What?" Lark asked.

Looking between her siblings, Shrike said, "Lisa told us what we had to do."

"Kill the host," Wren whispered.

"Kill? No." Lark shook her head. "No, we can't just kill Trent."

"We can't leave him to be consumed by that thing," Shrike said. "That's just torture. It's wrong."

Lark glanced at the strangers before dropping her voice to a breath, "So is murder."

"This isn't murder. It's mercy," Wren said. "Would you want to live with a demon inside of you?"

"I can do it on my own," Shrike said gently.

"No." Lark took the box back and cradled it close. "We started this as a family. We'll finish it the same way. It's what Dad would want."

# Chapter 7

Lark squirmed on the narrow bench seat, trying to find a comfortable position. It was impossible. Shrike's old pickup truck was built for function, not comfort. Its engine continued to work even as the frame rusted around it. Barely a few inches separated the back from the twin front seats and the top of Shrike's head almost hit the ceiling. Sighing, Lark repositioned her pillow under her head and hugged the small box of ashes to her stomach. It didn't help. She was so exhausted that she physically ached, but she couldn't sleep. It probably wouldn't be long before it was Wren's turn to rest anyway.

None of them had felt safe returning to a motel—even the decoy one. The demon had proven it could track them down. Instead, they had decided to aimlessly drive around the city, just killing time until daybreak. Streetlights and shadows flashed across the cab roof as they travelled along the highway. Lark settled into the seat and tried to let the familiarity relax her; the constant rumble of the engine, the overworked heater turning the air uncomfortably humid, the low static hum of the radio. Closing her eyes, she released a slow breath. She was finally drifting toward sleep when Shrike muttered a curse.

"What's wrong?" Wren asked.

Cracking one eye open, Lark watched Shrike take a hand off the wheel to rub her neck.

"What's wrong with your stitches?" Wren whispered.

"Nothing," Shrike said.

"You're bleeding again."

"Keep your voice down," Shrike said. "You'll wake Lark."

Wren sighed. "If you don't take care of them, you're going to get an infection. At least have a shower."

"I'm not going to a hotel room."

"Fine." He paused for a moment, and Lark could hear him tapping on his phone. "Take the next exit."

"Why?"

"Truck stop. Their website says they have showers. They look pretty clean."

"They charge you to use those," Shrike snapped.

"I will pay the twelve dollars," Wren said.

"I want snacks," Lark mumbled sleepily.

Shrike growled. "I told you to keep your voice down."

"I was already awake," Lark said.

Shrike snorted.

"Ah, there's the grunt of surrender." Wren chuckled.

Lark smiled, her eyes still closed. "She sounds like an angry bear."

"Lark, go to sleep," Shrike grumbled.

Lark closed her eyes again and smiled as her siblings continued to bicker. She was finally able to relax and began to inch toward sleep. A clawed hand grabbed her leg. Jerking upright with a gasp, she pressed her back against the door and pulled her knees to her chest, clutching the box of ashes tightly. Shrike had pulled into the truck stop and parked beneath its sign. Neon lights buzzed and a hazy blue glow filled the cab. It was still too dark. There were too many shadows.

"Wren?" Lark mumbled. "Shrike?"

The droning electrical buzz grew louder. Lark's gut squirmed.

"Guys?"

Lark looked to her siblings and found the front seats empty. The engine was off, the doors shut tight, and she was alone. All she could think was that she must have fallen asleep and lost track of time. Squeezing through the gap between the front seats, she stretched out. Shrike always left her notes trapped between the sun visors and the ceiling. Her shoulder ached as she hooked a finger around the driver's sun visor and flipped it down. There was nothing there.

"Oh, this is bad," she whispered to herself and glanced around.

The parking lot was quiet and cast in the blue hue.

"Shrike! Wren!"

A thick frost quickly spread across the windows and distorted her vision. Still gripping the box, she found her snow coat and rummaged into the pockets for her phone. Her panted breaths churned into fog as she hit the speed dial with her thumb. Each call rang out. Neither sibling answered. She couldn't even hear their phones ringing.

"Okay. Okay. I can handle this. I can find them."

Carefully tucking her father's remains into her backpack, she hid the bag under her pillow and pulled on her snow coat. Then she slipped into the front seat and peered out the windshield. The gas station was a blurry shape outline with neon lights. Mack trucks were parked in long, neat rows. Nothing moved. She twisted around but couldn't find a single person. It was even hard to tell where the highway was. The place was utterly deserted. Pressing a hand against her chest, Lark drew in a deep breath. Her heartbeat fluttered against her trembling fingertips.

"Still breathing," she whispered to herself.

With renewed confidence, she checked the ignition. The keys were gone. She looked to the door to find the old pull-up locks engaged. Lark took these as good signs. Wherever Shrike had gone, she had gone willingly and with enough time to make sure Lark was safe inside.

"Maybe she just forgot to leave a note. Right, Dad? I mean, we're all tired and stressed. It could have slipped her mind." Twisting around again, she tried to stop her hands from shaking. "So, where's Wren?"

She leaned against the wheel and struggled to get a decent look at the gas station. There was still nothing but colored lights and dark shadows. Her skin crawled. Squirming in the driver's seat, she pulled one leg up to her chest and drummed her fingers restlessly against her knee.

"It's probably safer in the truck. I should wait for them. They'll be back soon." Her fingers stilled. "But what if they're in trouble? What if they need my help and I'm just sitting here? Dad, what do you think I should do?"

Lark chewed on her bottom lip and waited for her father to give her a sign. No matter how many times she scanned the parking lot, nothing changed. Her phone remained heavy and silent in her pocket. There was only the buzz of the lights and the soft crack of growing frost. Without the heater, the cab swiftly grew unbearably cold. She shivered again and pulled the edges of her coat closer. Her feet were numb. Hugging her knee, she stared at the building.

"They're probably in there getting the snacks I asked for," Lark whispered. "Or maybe Shrike's having her shower, and that's why she's not answering. And you know how Wren gets. If something has caught his attention, he wouldn't even hear his phone. Wren probably wanted to keep an eye on her and didn't want to wake me, that's all. I bet they'd come running back the moment I leave to look for them."

The blue light couldn't completely illuminate the parking lot. There was no way to get to the building without entering the shadows.

"Dad, what should I do?"

She could almost hear him whisper for her to try calling again. Blood rushed through her ears, almost drowning out the repetitive ringing. Again, neither of them picked up. Sinking down into her coat, she kept her eyes locked on the truck stop. The shift of light happened so gradually that she didn't notice it at first. The building's interior lights stayed bright while all the others dimmed. Shadows thickened around the truck, and she knew she didn't have much longer to make her choice. Either she committed to waiting and let the darkness engulf her, or she made a mad dash to the gas station. The thought of being caught outside, alone, terrified her.

"I won't be alone. Not really. Shrike and Wren are out there. All I have to do is scream and they'll come running, just like always." Tears burned her eyes. "They won't leave me alone."

It struck her then that her siblings might be in the same situation. They could be alone out there, right now, desperately needing her to come and help them. Biting her lip, she turned to the door and grabbed the pull-up lock. She hesitated and carefully looked out each window again, rechecking for any hint of movement. Nothing. She cautiously unlocked the door and opened it. The world remained still and quiet, making her brave enough to jump down from the cab. Slamming the door closed, she glanced around. Everything was getting darker by the second, and a cold fog had started to rise. She started for the building. Her footsteps echoed as the light died. Hugging herself tightly, she picked up her pace. The building was farther away than she had estimated. The vehicles around her were taller and the shadows between them thicker. It seemed like the parking lot stretched out in every direction. There were hundreds of trucks and not a single sign of life.

"What the hell am I doing?" she gasped.

The stupidity of leaving Shrike's truck hit her like a physical blow. Spinning around, she intended to go back but froze in place. She had kept to a straight line. The truck should have been right behind her. But it was gone, replaced by a wall of semitrailers. Lark's panted breath misted before her. She twisted around in tight circles. There was no sign of the pickup. The shadows thickened and moved toward her like a solid wall. The truck stop was the only point of light, and she sprinted for it. Something followed her.

Heavy footsteps closed in behind her. She glanced back but couldn't see what it was. Jumping the curb, she finally reached the entrance. There was a soft ping and the electronic doors slowly parted. The footsteps were closer now. Lark tried to squeeze through the narrow gap. The doors stopped and the interior lights died. There was only the soft blue glow to break up the shadows. She shoved at the doors, but they wouldn't move. Wedged in the gap, she turned to face what was coming for her. The footsteps stopped. A figure emerged from the murky darkness. It wasn't anything more than a silhouette, but she knew him instantly.

"Daddy?" Lark sobbed. "Daddy, you've come back. I knew you would. I knew you wouldn't just leave us. If demons are real, why not ghosts?"

Lark yanked herself free of the doors and turned to face him fully. The blue light glistened off the tears that streaked his face.

"Don't cry," Lark said. "You're back now. You can haunt me for the rest of my life. Family sticks together, right? You'll see. We'll be happy, I promise."

He looked at her for a long moment before turning away.

"What are you doing?" Lark stammered.

While he stopped, the edges of his body began to gradually dissolve.

"No!" She ran to him. "Don't leave me! Daddy! Please don't leave!"

Finally, she was standing in front of him. Reaching up, Lark cupped her father's cheeks with trembling hands and tried to force him to be solid again. To be real. To hold her one more time so she could feel safe and treasured.

"Stay with me." Tears burned her eyes and blurred her vision. "I can't do this without you. None of us can, Daddy. We need you. Please. Stay."

There was a flush of victory and relief when he solidified into flesh and bone.

"Thank you," Lark whispered. "See? I knew you could do it."

She squeezed a little harder and his skin split open; unleashing spurts of blood as he began to rot.

"No. No, please."

His once-tender eyes shriveled and blackened. His lips peeled back from his gums to form a grotesque smile. Decay bloated his body until the skin grew slick and dangled from his bones. His jaw dropped open, his nose caved in, and his skull began to crack apart. The tighter she held him, the more the bones shifted. The rotted sludge that was once his brain oozed between the shards.

"Daddy, please," she whimpered. "Please don't make me see this."

This was why they had cremated him. To spare him the brutal realities of death. She hadn't been able to stomach the idea of him rotting in his grave, cold and alone.

The shredded remains of his throat trembled as he rasped, "Run."

She dropped to her knees, keeping with him as he crumpled. Her hands darted across his face, trying to piece him back together but only breaking him more. Rancid sludge slicked her fingers.

"Run."

Fire ripped through him. She saw the flames an instant before he exploded into ash. The remains fell over her in a dark cloud. As it settled around her, she spotted the colossal creature standing at the edge of the darkness, barely visible, its eyes burning like embers. She met its gaze and felt its sadistic glee. Then it attacked her.

\*\*\*

Shrike glanced in the rearview mirror. "Lark? Lark!"

Wren flinched and looked up from his laptop. His confusion vanished when he finally noticed Lark's low whimpering.

"I think she's having a nightmare," Shrike said.

He closed his laptop and hell broke out. Lark screamed and thrashed. She pummeled the seats and kicked at the ceiling. Her snow boot stomped down on the side of Shrike's neck. Doubling over in blinding pain, she swerved into oncoming traffic. A distant horn blared as she pulled the truck back into her lane.

"Shrike?" Wren gasped.

"I'm okay."

Wren unclicked his seat belt and pushed between the seats.

"Wake her up!" Shrike ordered.

"I'm trying!"

"Then pin her down!"

Wren thumped against Shrike's side as he squirmed into the back. The constant push sent them careening into the oncoming lane. The Mack truck was closer now and its headlights blinded her. Yanking hard on the wheel, they bounced over the curb and into the parking lot. She stomped on the brakes. The back wheels hit a patch of black ice, and they spun out. Shrike battled with the wheel until they jerked to a stop. The siblings stayed silent as the truck rocked on its suspension.

Shrike gasped. "Is anyone hurt?"

"No," Wren said.

Lark stifled a sob.

"What the hell happened?" Shrike asked.

"Where's Dad? I dropped him. Where did he go?" Lark rambled and wept.

Shrike undid her seat belt. By the time she shifted around, Wren had already found the box. Lark clutched it to her chest and curled her entire body around it. Looking desperately to Shrike, Wren drew his sister into a tight hug.

"Lark?" Shrike asked softly.

Wren rubbed Lark's trembling shoulders. "You were dreaming. It was just a nightmare."

"No. No, I wasn't. It was the demon."

"You fell asleep. That's all," Shrike said.

"No!" Lark snapped. "Listen to me! It was the demon. It got into my dreams. It made me watch."

"Watch what?" Wren asked.

Lark pressed her forehead against her knees and wailed, a gut-wrenching sound that left Shrike trembling. Her little sister had only made that sound once before—the night they had found their father. Wren tightened his grip on her, rocking with her and rubbing soothing circles over her back.

"You're safe. We've got you," he whispered. "Take a deep breath for me. No, none of that gasping. Come on. Follow me."

Wren drew in a long, slow lungful. Eventually, Lark mimicked him, and her wails gradually ebbed into small whimpers.

"There you go." He smiled weakly.

"It was the demon," Lark insisted.

"We believe you." Wren met Shrike's gaze. "I've come across the concept in my research. A lot of people believe demons can invade dreams."

"Maybe that's how it keeps finding us. Maybe it can track our dreams," Shrike said.

"Do you think we should keep moving?" Wren asked.

"We were when she was dreaming," Shrike replied. "Would it know we've stopped?"

"Lark," Wren said gently. "We need you to tell us what you experienced."

Lark pressed her head against her knees. "It made me see Dad rot."

Images flashed across Shrike's mind and her stomach heaved.

"It made sure I knew I was alone. Ever since Dad—" She cut herself off and swallowed. "I never thought I'd be without him. I know that's silly. Children are supposed to outlive their parents. But he was Dad. Joe Rose. How can the world exist without *Joe Rose*?"

"We both feel the same way," Wren said.

"I'm not even sure who I am without him," Shrike confessed.

They fell silent and flinched when Lark gasped.

"Shrike, you're bleeding!"

"God, I completely forgot," Wren said. "Let me take a look."

"I'm fine."

"Shrike." Wren sighed.

"We need to figure this out."

"I can tell Wren everything while you have a shower," Lark cut in. "I'm okay now. Don't look at me like that. I said *okay*, not *great*. Besides, you always take quick showers. I bet we won't even have time to finish our coffees before you're out."

"You need to take care of yourself," Wren added.

"Your hair is horrible, and you smell like garlic," Lark said.

"Well, you're sounding better," Shrike mumbled.

"It's like Dad always said," Lark said. "Before you walk through hell, sit and have a beer."

"A little bit of normalcy will help us feel in control," Wren agreed.

"Fine." Shrike flopped into her seat and turned the engine on.

It was never fair when they ganged up against her. Shrike forced the truck into gear before placing a hand against her chest.

"Still breathing," she mumbled.

Wren and Lark replied in unison, "Still breathing."

Shrike finally took a proper look around. The parking lot was huge. Neat rows of Mack trucks were parked to one side of the storefront. The rest of the area was empty except for small piles of dirty snow. People braved the cold to smoke and there were plenty more inside. It wasn't crowded but clearly popular with long-haul truckers. Shrike parked close to the storefront, grabbed her bag from the flatbed, and waited for her siblings to get organized.

Shrike scanned the area as they crossed the brightly lit parking lot. They were mostly ignored apart from a homeless man huddled under the blazing "welcome" sign. His bloodshot eyes locked onto Lark and stretched wide.

"Hey," he hissed. "Hey, pretty girl. Look at me."

Shrike positioned herself to block the man's view. He clicked his fingers and tongue but didn't try to get closer. The building was stifling hot. Shrike began to sweat, and the traces of salt made her neck sting. The gas station shared the building with a convenience store and a fast-food place she had never heard of. The showers were in the back. It was an automatic setup with the door codes printed on the receipts the machine spat out. Shrike was relieved to see a cleaner lazily moving from one room to another.

"Hey."

The siblings turned to see the homeless man blocking the entrance. He wiggled his dirt-smeared fingers at Lark like she was a dog he was trying to coax closer.

"Hey, pretty girl. Come here."

Shrike bared her teeth. "Stay away from my sister."

The man kept his eyes on Lark and whistled. "Here, pretty girl. Come on. Good girl."

Wren grabbed Shrike's arm, keeping her from stalking toward the man.

"Go take a shower," he said. "I'll keep close to Lark. We'll be fine."

The man finally looked at Shrike. Holding her gaze, he backed out of the building. The electronic doors closed and he continued to stare at them through the glass. Wren tugged on Shrike's arm until she looked at him. He motioned to the back of the store. Reluctantly, she obeyed. The late hour was a small blessing. She didn't have to wait long before her number was called. She was so exhausted that the keypad blurred as she punched in the code. With a low buzz, the door unlocked and the interior light flicked on. Shrike slumped the instant the exhaust fan started up. She wanted steam and heat and a warmth that she could feel to her bones. Otherwise, the room was what she had expected. Small and narrow. A shower stall at the back. A toilet and sink closer to the door.

Dumping her bag on the counter, she stripped off her clothes, grabbed her nailbrush, and slumped into the shower. Goosebumps crept over her skin as she waited for the water to heat up. The following shiver made her entire body ache. She was a bit too tall for the showerhead and had to stoop to scrub the complimentary soap into her hair. Even after she had rubbed her skin raw, she didn't feel clean. Dried blood stained the water pink as she discovered new bruises. Carefully, she washed her stitches, vaguely aware that she had lost track of the days. It was possible that they still needed to be kept dry. Washing off the suds, she heard a metallic click. Someone was rattling the door handle.

"Lark?" Shrike called over the pelting shower. "Wren?"

The door rattled violently but the lock held. Shrike turned off the shower and quietly crept out of the stall.

"Someone's in here!" she said.

The exhaust fan sucked out the steam and dried the water on her skin. Shivering, she inched closer to the door and called again. The handle stilled. She waited a few seconds longer before grabbing a towel from her bag and half-heartedly wiped herself off. Every so often, she thought she heard a low croaking whisper, but it always faded when she stopped to listen.

Shrike dug in her bag for something to wear and cursed. She had completely forgotten that she had crammed the garlic bulb necklace into her bag. The smell had seeped into everything. Pulling on sweatpants and sports bra, she leaned over the counter to inspect her seeping stitches. Pain sliced up her neck and made her scream. Gripping the sink, she clamped a hand over the side of her neck. Icy fingers pushed through the stitches and scraped against her palm. Shrike jerked her hand away. Nothing was there. The bleeding had stopped, and her skin was raw, but it all looked normal. She tapped the stitches and winced.

Teeth clamped onto her back and bit down until they scraped against her shoulder blade. Her knees buckled. Slumped against the counter, she choked on her screams and reached over her shoulder. Nothing was there but her back was slick with blood. The puckered skin of the bite mark split under her touch. Icy teeth drove deeper into her flesh, so cold that they burned. Something was inside of her. It squirmed and pushed against her fingertips. Pain whited out her vision as she dug her fingers into the bite. There was too much blood. She couldn't get a good grip on the object. Using her other hand to open the skin, she shoved her fingers deeper. Her nails hooked around the edges of the object, and she pulled. It popped free, and she screamed. Blinking away tears, she looked down. A human tooth lay on her trembling palm. She flinched back and it clattered into the sink. The other phantom teeth continued to gnaw into her shoulder blade. Thrashing, she clawed at the broken skin, frantically trying to pry them out. The door handle rattled again. When the lock held, someone began to pound against the door.

"Hey!" a voice rasped. "You've got to get her out! Get her out!"

Blood slicked the tiles. Shrike lost her footing, her head cracked against the wall, and toppled to the ground. White dots danced across her vision.

"Got to get her!" the man outside bellowed. "Are you listening to me? You've got to get her now!"

There was too much blood. Too much pain. She could barely move.

"Got to get her!"

The teeth tore their way out of her skin. She could feel them wiggling. Crawling forward, she grabbed the counter and tried to drag herself up. Her bag was in the way. It slid off the counter and dropped onto her, spilling its contents across the wet floor. Suddenly, the pain stopped. Aftershocks made her twitch as she lay sprawled over the floor. The ringing in her ears almost drowned out the constant banging against the door. Swallowing thickly, she pushed aside the scattered clothes and garlic necklace and sat up. The back of her skull throbbed so hard that her stomach rolled.

"It's found her," a voice rasped from the other side of the door. He hit the keypad until the electronic lock screeched.

"What the hell are you doing, Robby?" a new voice snapped.

"Fine! I'll save her myself!"

It was quiet for a moment, just long enough for Shrike to get to her feet. Then someone gently knocked on the door.

"He's gone now," the new voice said. "You're okay. You can come out."

Shrike turned to see her back in the mirror. A dark bruise surrounded the bite mark on her shoulder. Clean water drizzled down her back. There wasn't any blood. Not on her or anywhere else in the room. It was all just water.

"Are you okay?" the stranger asked. "Look, if you don't respond, I'm going to have to unlock the door."

Shrike cradled her head. "I'm fine."

Lark's scream made her blood run cold. Shrike rushed to the door, yanked it open, and shoved the stunned employee aside.

"Lark!"

People began to shout and crowd together. Wren raced across her field of vision, rushing to the entrance.

"Shrike!" Wren bellowed. "He's got Lark!"

# Chapter 8

Wren shoved through the thin crowd. People had gathered to cut off the homeless man's exit, keeping him from escaping into the darkness with Lark. He had one arm locked around her neck and brandished a kitchen knife with the other. He slashed at anyone who ventured too close.

"Take it easy, Robby," an employee said as he inched closer. "What are you doing, man?"

"I'm saving her. No one else was going to do it. I have to do everything," the homeless man said.

"But she's safe here, Robby," the employee pressed.

"She's not. I told her to leave but she wouldn't. No one listens to me!"

The people crowded around Wren, forcing him to squeeze his way to the front. Lark met his gaze with wide eyes. She gripped Robby's arm with both hands, pulling hard enough to keep him from choking her.

"I'm sorry," she said meekly. "I didn't mean to upset you."

Robby's face softened. "Oh, you're okay, pretty girl. I'll take good care of you."

He cut off to slash at a trucker that had tried to creep up behind him. The stranger backed up, and the crowd grumbled.

"You're scaring her," Wren said.

"I'm not what she should be scared of!" Robby screamed.

The crowd surged forward. Wren was crushed between huge men twice his size. In the chaos, an elbow cracked against his nose. White-hot pain pulsated across his face and his eyes watered. Half blind, he staggered and bumped into a few people, barely able to keep upright. Tension simmered through the crowd. The doors opened and a few more people came in, further cutting off his exit.

"Robby," the employee stammered. "You're not going to get out of here with her. Just relax, okay?"

"I didn't want to do this," Robby shot back.

A few of the larger men rushed forward. Robby forced them back with wild swipes of the knife. Lark pulled against him, almost slipping free. Robby pulled her back at the last moment.

"Leave us alone!" Robby screamed. "I know what I'm doing! Just back off and let me do it!"

Lark's eyes darted around. Suddenly, she unleashed an earsplitting scream that made everyone flinch away. Shrike took advantage of the shock to burst out of the crowd and tackle Robby to the ground. Lark fell with them. The tension snapped, and everyone rushed in at once. Wren managed to keep upright through the first few jolts but ended up losing his footing. He curled into a tight ball, trying to protect himself from the people that ran past and over him. It was over in an instant. Wincing in pain, he lifted his head, looking through the clustered legs. He caught sight of Lark first. She had been pulled away from Robby and thrown onto the ground.

"Lark!"

She turned toward him. Their eyes met an instant before she was yanked out of sight. He still heard her over the combined shouts.

"Stop Shrike!"

"Shrike?" Wren's stomach dropped. "Oh, no."

He could only catch quick glimpses of Shrike. Blood splatted her face and coated her knuckles.

"Hey, that's enough," someone said.

"He's down. Let him go!" another shouted.

The employee tried to force their way to the center of the crowd. "She's going to kill him! Stop her!"

"Shrike!" Wren pushed forward but wasn't strong enough to move anyone aside. "Let me through! She's my sister! I can help!"

Someone blindly shoved him aside.

"I can stop her!"

The lie tasted bitter. Their father was always the one who could talk sense to her. He was always there to rein her in. *Dad's dead,* Wren thought. *I'm the oldest. I'm supposed to take care of them.* Horrified, he realized that he had lost sight of them both.

"Lark! Shrike!" Neither of them answered. He couldn't breathe. "Where are my sisters?!"

Wren had just scrambled into a crouch when darkness slipped across his peripheral vision. A shadow went unnoticed as it slithered around the people's legs. Strong arms sprung from the formless mass. A head followed. One with small glowing eyes and a mouth full of mangled teeth. The creature met Wren's gaze, grinned, and snaked to the side. He glimpsed Lark's boots before losing sight of them both. Lark screamed his name, and he shot to his feet. He couldn't find her. He couldn't help them.

"Lark?"

Blue and red lights flashed over the mob. The electronic doors opened, allowing in a gust of frigid air and the wail of a police siren.

"Back off!" an authoritative voice bellowed through a bullhorn. "Everyone, back off now!"

Wren froze. He knew that voice. "It can't be."

Everyone shuffled back from the doors, spreading out enough that he could see Barsotti cross the threshold, flanked by three other uniformed officers. One of them pushed forward, clearly trying to take control of the situation. Almost everyone kept their eyes on Barsotti.

"What happened to Ruckus Robby?" Barsotti demanded.

"The blonde," the employee replied.

Shrike straightened and emerged above the others. Dripping with sweat and blood, she looked almost feral. But she was alive. Wren buried his hands in his hair and heaved a sigh in relief.

"Of course, it's you," Barsotti said. Before the other officers could comment, he continued, "Where are the others?"

Shrike glared at him. He rolled his eyes and spoke into the bullhorn.

"Listen up. Anyone that doesn't want to make friends with cops tonight better leave now. Everyone else, grab a coffee and take a seat. We'll be doing the rounds."

"This is completely against regulations," one of the officers said.

Barsotti ignored him. "Rose siblings, we're going to have a chat."

***

Shrike curled her bare toes against the tiles and tried to sit still. Barsotti had forced them to sit at one of the circular tables before the younger officer had dragged him away. The two of them had been arguing since. Shrike absently rubbed at her aching knuckles and glanced to the far side of the room. Robby, the homeless man, winced as one of the officers tended to his broken lip. She hadn't done nearly as much damage as she had wanted to.

"Why did you scream?"

Lark's question made Shrike flinch. "Huh?"

"When you were in the shower," Lark said. "I heard you scream."

"Oh. I thought I saw something."

Wren huffed. "Aren't we past this? Just tell us."

"We don't have time to get into it."

"I saw a shadow demon," Wren confessed. "It was in the crowd. It smiled at me."

Shrike met his gaze. "The cuts on my shoulder grew teeth."

They fell silent as a policeman strolled near their table. Eventually, he moved on, and Lark whispered.

"You're right. We should get into the details later. Right now, we just need to get out of here."

"Barsotti isn't going to let us go easily. He looks eager to drag us back to the station," Wren said.

"Why is he constantly showing up?" Shrike grumbled. She shook her head. "Lark, what happened? Why did that man grab you?"

"It's my fault," Wren said. "I thought I had scared him off. Then he just rushed up behind her—"

Lark curled up against his side. "You can't blame yourself. The man is clearly unhinged. And it all happened so fast."

"I was useless. You both needed me, and I did nothing," Wren said. "God, I'm so sorry."

"Wren, stop it. You couldn't have known," Lark said.

His shoulders tensed. "But *it* did. I think it might have set it up somehow."

"What do you mean?" Shrike asked.

"Don't take this the wrong way," he said. "But I'm the oldest. And now that Dad's... gone, I'm the man of the family. He would want me to look after you guys. The demon forced Lark to see what she fears. Being alone. Seeing Dad like that. Well, I've been terrified that I'm not good enough to keep you safe. That this thing is going to kill you guys, and I won't be able to do anything but watch. I've never felt so useless as I did just then."

Lark pulled Wren into a tight hug. "You're not useless. You're a great big brother."

"Thanks." Wren sniffed and pulled back. "If it is using our fears against us, how does teeth fit in?"

Shrike's knee jumped. "I don't know. But I couldn't handle feeling it moving inside of me. If I had a knife, I would have cut it out. I was completely out of control."

"You can't be serious!" one of the officers snarled. He glared around the room and dropped his voice. "This is why you got demoted."

"Probably," Barsotti said dismissively. He spun on his heel and walked toward the siblings.

"We're not done yet."

"Jackson, just write me up," Barsotti said without looking back.

He got to the table, dropped into an empty chair, and started scribbling in his notepad. The siblings glanced at each other, trying to decide what to do. Seconds stretched into minutes. Shrike watched the officers talk to each of the witnesses in turn. Robby was given a coffee and an ice pack.

"Aren't you going to arrest him?" Shrike snapped.

"Who? Ruckus Robby? Nah. He didn't mean any harm."

"He had a knife," Shrike said.

"For self-defense."

"He tried to kill my sister."

"He wasn't going to kill her," Barsotti said. "But from what I've heard, you were definitely trying to kill him."

"I can't believe this."

"Relax," Barsotti said. "We have other things to talk about."

Shrike bit the inside of her cheeks. She wanted to grab her brother and sister and run. Barsotti made her hesitate. It seemed like he was baiting her with his silence, trying to provoke her into doing something stupid. Something he could use against them. Every unexplained event fueled his obsession.

Pressing her thumb against her bruised knuckles, she thoughtlessly asked, "Are you stalking us?"

Barsotti stopped writing and arched an eyebrow at her.

"It's a big city. How are you *always* around?" Shrike demanded.

"This is a highway truck stop. You're on my turf." Before she could reply, he swept his eyes over her. "Aren't you cold? Where's your jacket?"

"In the bathroom." Shrike defiantly crossed her arms over her chest and glared at him. "Can I go get it?"

"I'll have someone grab it for you." He called across the room to another officer before adding, "Nice outfit by the way."

"Shrike," Wren warned.

She swallowed her rage and stayed silent.

Barsotti's gaze flicked between the siblings before he sighed and returned to writing in his notepad. "Who bit you?"

"You know who," Shrike said tensely. "You were there."

"Lisa only got your neck. Not your back."

"Prove it," she said.

His eyes flicked to her, and she snapped her mouth shut. *He's always around.* She had been convinced that the demon had mimicked him that night at the hotel to lure her out. But now, she had to question if he had been there, if he was somehow involved. *How much does he know?*

"Shrike?" Barsotti pressed.

Snapped out of her thoughts, she said, "I don't remember."

His brow furrowed. "You don't remember what?"

"Um."

Wren and Lark both stared at her with wide eyes.

"I don't remember," she repeated.

"That's not suspicious," Barsotti mumbled, finished what he was writing, and turned to Wren and Lark. "What about you two? Do you remember how she got bit?"

"Lark was attacked. Perhaps we should focus on that," Wren said.

Officer Jackson stormed to the table and shoved Shrike's jacket toward her. He glared at Barsotti with disgust.

"I'm going on the record to say that you're going completely against regulations."

"Are you sure? There's an awful lot of rules," Barsotti replied.

"This isn't a joke. They need to be questioned separately and the perpetrator needs—"

"Leave Robby alone, Jackson." Barsotti waved the homeless man over and his voice softened. "Do you have something you want to say?"

Robby hunched his shoulders. "I didn't mean to scare the pretty girl. I was just trying to keep her safe."

"You held her at knifepoint to keep her safe?" Jackson asked.

"She was being followed."

Jackson straightened. "By whom?"

"Her shadow. It was following her everywhere."

"He's insane," Jackson hissed at Barsotti.

Barsotti shrugged. "Well, he's not wrong."

"I tried to warn her," Robby cut in. "I even told the big one, but she wouldn't come out of the bathroom. And the one with glasses wasn't much help. I had to save her."

"You assaulted her," Jackson said.

"And he apologizes. Don't you, Robby?" Barsotti fixed the homeless man with a meaningful look.

"Oh, right, yeah. I do. I'm sorry. I hope I didn't scare you, little miss."

Lark gaped at him, clearly not sure what to say to that. Barsotti broke the standoff by handing Robby a few dollars.

"Go get yourself something to eat. I'll give you a lift to the shelter once I'm done."

Robby scoffed. "Are you nuts? All the shelters are full for the winter. Even if I could get a bunk, I don't want to be stuck with those jerks. They steal. And you cops never do anything about it."

"It's too cold to be on the streets. Let me give you a few more bucks so you can at least ride the bus tonight."

Robby shrunk back, his eyes wide and his lips trembling. "Nah, nah, no one rides the bus anymore. It's all those damn shadows. They're all wrong. People get on and they don't get off. I told you lot about it. Not that you do anything."

Shrike's stomach dropped. *People get on the bus, and they don't get off.* She glanced to her siblings and saw the same muted horror.

"I'm okay staying here," Robby insisted. "They let me hang around. I won't cause any more trouble. I promise."

"You're coming—"

"They're not pressing charges against him," Barsotti cut Jackson off. "Robby, why don't you go grab a shower? We'll talk later."

The old man shuffled off the instant he had the extra cash in hand.

Jackson turned to Lark. "You can press charges. He assaulted you."

"They're not going to," Barsotti said. "The Rose siblings don't like attention. They're not going to put their names on legal paperwork."

"That's it. You've pushed your luck too far this time. I'm reporting you."

Barsotti smiled as another uniformed officer hurried over. Grabbing Jackson's arm, the officer dragged him a few steps away. It wasn't quite enough distance to get them out of earshot.

"Let it go, Jackson"

"He can't—"

"He can," the officer said. "Barsotti's sunk as low as he's allowed to."

"What does that mean?" Jackson whispered harshly.

Shrike glanced at Barsotti, finding him writing on his small notepad again, his jaw clenched tight.

"It means back off if you like your job." The officer dragged Jackson too far away for Shrike to hear any more of the conversation.

She glanced at her siblings. They nodded. They had heard it too.

"What were they talking about?" Shrike asked.

For once, Barsotti kept his mouth shut.

"Why do you get away with so much?" she pressed.

"Don't worry about it," Barsotti dismissed.

Shrike scoffed.

"Leave it, Shrike." Barsotti glared at her with an intensity that left her breathless. The rage dissipated with a smile. "We should focus on what is going on with you and your siblings."

"Lark is the victim here," Wren said.

"I don't care!" His hand shook as he roughly scrubbed at his face. "I need to understand. I need to make it stop."

"Make what stop?" Lark asked softly.

Barsotti clamped a hand over his mouth, his fingers digging into his stubble-covered cheek. When he stilled, Shrike realized how haggard he was. There were new lines on his face, darkness under his eyes, and a dusting of gray at his temples. It was like he had aged years in the few days they had known him.

"Barsotti." Lark reached across the small table to touch his shoulder. "Talk to me. What's happened to you?"

Only his eyes moved. He studied her for a long second before finally dropping his hand.

"Barsotti!" Jackson snapped from across the room.

Jerking, he blinked rapidly, sucked in a sharp breath, and forced a smile. "I'll be right with you."

"We need you right now, Barsotti."

Barsotti glanced around the table. "Stay."

The siblings watched him get up and walk toward the others. The instant he was out of earshot, they leaned against the table.

"Are you okay with this, Lark?" Shrike whispered. "Jackson is right. We can press charges."

"Barsotti's right. We can't handle the attention," Lark countered.

"We can make it work if this is something you need."

"Shrike, I'm okay, I promise. He barely gave me a scratch."

"Guys." Wren discreetly motioned to the clustered police officers. "I love you both, but we don't have time for this. We need to decide what we're going to do about Barsotti. He's not going to let this go."

"You saw him," Shrike said. "He looks like hell. The demon's tormenting him too."

"Unless it's prepping him," Wren said.

"Prepping him?" Lark asked.

"For possession," Wren said. "It seems like the demon picked Trent because he had access to victims."

"Robby said that homeless people have been going missing," Shrike mused.

"I'm not saying that I understand everything that's going on, or how demons pick their victims," Wren continued. "But if I was a demon looking for a meat suit, I'd pick the cop over the bus driver. It's obviously already got him in his sights."

"He is looking bad," Lark said. "But maybe it's just torturing him."

Shrike shook her head. "We can't risk it. Look at how much he gets away with now. And that other guy all but said he's protected. Imagine what a demon could do if it gets inside him."

Lark paled. "How do we stop it? The salt didn't work."

"Wait." Wren straightened. "What did it say when it crossed the line? Something about it not being a ghost."

"That means something to you?" Shrike asked.

"I need my laptop," Wren said as his brain worked too fast for his mouth to keep up. "It's in my research file. There was a type of magic that used salt to repel ghosts but admitted that it had no effect on demons."

"Why didn't you mention that earlier?" Lark asked.

"Because they literally called it *magic*. Besides, all the rest of it was insane. It was like they were raiding their pantry. It was all herbs and spices. I need my laptop."

He squirmed in his seat, eyeing the door like he might make a run for it.

"Wren," Shrike snapped. "Focus."

"Right. Sorry." He still didn't look away from the door. "Garlic. Yes, I'm sure that was it. Salt to repel ghosts, garlic to repel demons." Wren turned to Lark with a smirk. "See why I didn't pay attention to it?"

Lark gasped. "Okay, so, the demon bit Shrike but ran away when she fell into a display of garlic. And it left you alone after you grabbed the garlic necklace, right? So maybe there is something to it."

"Maybe. Or maybe it's just setting us up. Letting us think we know its weakness so it can get the upper hand. We've already lost the element of surprise. Trent will be prepared for us this time. We can't mess up again," Shrike said.

"It's not like we can test any of our theories," Lark whispered.

Wren slumped, and Shrike rubbed at her dry eyes.

"Why do I feel like we're right back where we started?" Lark asked.

Shrike twisted in her seat to stare at Barsotti. "Do you think he knows he's getting stalked by a demon? Maybe he's pieced together more than we have. He's got more resources."

"Maybe," Lark said. "We all saw the shadows at the mental hospital at least."

"Lisa." Shrike turned back around. "She told us how to fix this.

She's the most reliable source we've got."

"She just said that they were all supposed to die," Lark dismissed. A split second later, she understood. "He has to die."

Wren looked between them. "Lisa said that they had to die like they were supposed to. Like they would have if we hadn't interfered. Trent was supposed to die in a house fire. We have to burn him."

The siblings looked at each other, each one willing the others to suggest a different course of action. Shrike was the one to voice it.

"We have to kill him."

"We can't," Lark whispered.

"We can't leave the demon alone. We can't contain it. We can't extract it from Trent." Wren said it all without a hint of emotion. "What other choice do we have?"

"We are jumping to murder disturbingly quickly. And not just that." She dropped her voice into a hiss. "You want to *burn* him."

"I don't want to," Wren snapped. "But what else can we do?"

"You know it killed those missing homeless people," Shrike said.

Lark opened her mouth to argue but said nothing.

"None of us *want* to do this," Shrike said.

"Who else will stop it if we don't?" Wren mumbled.

"We have to do this, Lark."

"And we all need to agree to it. We all share the blame." Wren cleared his throat. "We all share the guilt."

Each sibling nodded in turn. Not knowing what else to say, Shrike looked around the truck stop. There was barely a hint that something violent had happened. The four officers sipped coffee while they talked. A few people stood scattered around the store, waiting for the officers to return and continue the interviews. Beyond that, customers came and went, served by bored employees. Shrike had to wonder how often they had to experience violent outbursts to accept them so easily.

"So, exactly how are we going to do this?" Shrike asked.

# Chapter 9

Lark shivered as she stepped outside. Hours in the overheated truck stop had made her forget how bitterly cold the early mornings were in this city. The highway was busier now, and the parking lot was starting to fill with truckers in desperate need of a caffeine fix. The row of Mack trucks that now blocked their view of the car park were coated in a fresh dusting of snow. Lark lifted one mitten-covered hand and watched the tiny snowflakes catch on the colorful wool.

"Does anyone have eyes on Barsotti?" Shrike whispered, scanning a cluster of uniformed officers in the distance.

"Yeah, we should thank him," Lark said.

"Thank him for what?" Shrike asked

"He stopped you from assaulting a cop," Wren pointed out. "I don't think Jackson would've been so forgiving."

After his talk with the other officer, Jackson had kept his distance from Barsotti, but he had still pushed hard for Ruckus Robby to face charges. No one else had been interested. Lark had admired Jackson's persistence. The truck stop was apparently popular with traffic cops and there was a constant stream of officers coming and going. Jackson had approached a lot of them as they came in. People Lark assumed outranked Barsotti. She never got to hear any of their conversations, but they clearly didn't go the way Jackson had hoped. The man did not handle rejection well. When Barsotti had left the table, Jackson had swooped in and insisted that Lark press charges. His anger had fed Shrike's. It had dissolved into a screaming match. Barsotti had dragged Jackson away an instant before Shrike had swung. Lark hadn't seen either of the officers since.

"I still don't trust him," Shrike muttered.

"Bye-bye, pretty girl!"

The siblings turned to see Robby settled back in his place under the neon sign.

"You two take care of her now," Robby said cheerfully.

Lark grabbed Shrike's hand and tugged. With a disgusted grunt, Shrike reluctantly started walking again. Lark snatched up Wren's hand too, and they headed for the parking lot. For an instant, it was like they were back home, happy and carefree. Back when they were little. Before Dad started getting visions and everything got so complicated and dark. Lark closed her eyes and reveled in the memories.

"Are you sure you're all right?" Wren waited until Lark looked at him before adding, "It must have been scary."

"After being in Trent's house, Robby was nothing," Lark said.

Wren shrugged one shoulder. "We went into Trent's house expecting something to happen. We were supposed to be safe here. I was supposed to keep you safe."

"Hey," Lark said. "None of this is your fault. I'm fine. Barely a scratch. And we have other things to worry about."

They hadn't been able to discuss their plans. Someone always drifted too close every time they tried to get into the particulars. At least three hours of constantly halting debate and all they had managed to agree upon was that they needed to hit Trent just after a night shift.

Shrike took the lead as they squeezed between two trucks. "We should surprise him at the bus depot."

"The very public bus depot?" Lark asked.

"There wouldn't be a lot of people around at that hour. And we can time it. Hit him just before a train pulls out. Then most people will be down in the subway," Shrike said. "Besides, we can do it in the bus lockup, with a wire fence separating us from bystanders."

"Don't you remember all the floodlights? That place is lit up. We'll be spotted for sure," Lark said.

"But there'll be fewer shadows for the demon to play with," Shrike countered.

Wren gave a thoughtful hum. "Trent does seem to like working in the dark. At his house, he snuffed out the fire. Chances are, once he knows we're there, he'll cut the lights somehow."

"That could also work in our favor," Shrike said. "The power going out will create some confusion and knock out the security cameras."

"Oh, there will be a lot of security cameras," Lark said. "We'll end up on a most wanted list."

Shrike snorted. "For one murder and a little bit of arson?"

"Okay, maybe not the most wanted. But police will take an interest," Lark said.

"I'm sure they'd focus on putting the fire out before they bother to check the cameras. We can be out of town before they get their act together," Shrike said.

"About using fire," Lark said meekly. "What if he puts it out like he did at his house?"

"I guess we'll have to make sure he burns hotter than a wood fire," Wren said. "We'll need plenty of fuel."

"All the buses in the depot will have gas in their tanks," Shrike noted.

"Wait. So, we're setting the vehicles on fire now?" Lark asked.

Shrike paused and frowned. "What did you think I was talking about? Yes, we're setting them on fire."

"That's going to draw a lot of attention," Lark said. "How are we supposed to get away without everyone noticing?"

"Well, the fire will draw a lot of attention," Shrike teased.

Wren used his free hand to get his phone out of his pocket. "We can time it, like Shrike said. Hit just before a train leaves and get on board."

"Would the train still run?" Shrike asked.

"It makes sense that they'll try to evacuate the area. Besides, the depot is a transportation hub. If the trains stop, we still have cars, buses, taxis." He paused to study his phone screen. "By the street maps, we could even make it out on foot if we had to."

"What the hell are you doing in my truck?!" Shrike's sudden

outburst made Lark jump.

She looked around Shrike's body and spotted their flatbed truck. A man was leaning through the open passenger door.

"Shrike, don't," Lark said.

"Hey!" Shrike stormed forward, her whole body vibrating with rage. "Are you listening to me?!"

Lark tightened her grip on her sister's hand and tried to pull her back. Shrike didn't seem to notice that she was dragging the dead weight of her sibling across the parking lot.

"Hi, Barsotti!" Lark yelled with forced cheer.

"Hi, Lark," the man in the truck replied.

Shrike stopped. "How did you know it was him?"

"How did you not?" Lark replied.

"Shrike, hang back with me," Wren whispered.

Each sibling let go of Lark's hands and let her take a minimal lead.

"Weird coincidence," Lark said cheerfully as she came to stand by the open door. "This is our truck."

"Not a coincidence," Barsotti said.

"Oh?"

"That's why I'm searching it." He paused long enough to find Shrike. "You stand over there."

Shrike clenched her teeth and planted her feet. It took Wren pushing on her stomach with both hands to get her to move to the place Barsotti had indicated.

"Don't you need a warrant?" Lark asked.

"Nope."

"I'm pretty sure you do," Lark pressed, with a smile.

"Probable cause says I don't."

Lark giggled sweetly. "We look suspicious to you?"

Barsotti climbed out of the truck and stared at her for a second. He looked exhausted and completely un-charmed.

"Why don't you go stand with your sister?" he suggested.

Reaching in, he opened the glove box and began to rummage

through the random items stored there.

"How'd you get blood on the front seat?" Barsotti asked, almost like an afterthought.

"My stitches leaked," Shrike said between clenched teeth.

Barsotti glanced at her. "That's it? You just leaked?"

"Yes."

He heaved a sigh, pulled a pen light out of his jacket pocket, and trained the narrow beam over the interior. "I'm not calling you a liar, but that splatter pattern is."

"She pulled off her scarf," Wren cut in. "She was a bit rough. That probably caused the splatter."

"Right. So what's with all the blood in the flatbed?" Barsotti grabbed a handful of papers from the glove box and flipped through them. "That's the thing with old trucks. It's so hard to clean out all the cracks in the paintwork."

"I fish," Shrike replied. "I gut them in the back. Like you said, the paintwork holds onto it."

"Fish?"

Shrike clenched her jaw so tightly that Lark thought she was going to crack a tooth.

"Yeah. You'll find last year's permit in there."

"Ah, here it is." He flicked through the sheets again. "No old hunting permit? I would have pegged you for the type that loves to go shoot Bambi in the face."

Lark glanced back at her siblings. Wren already had a death grip on Shrike's bicep. They both knew she wasn't going to hold onto her temper much longer.

"We don't like venison," Lark said. "Plus, she makes amazing barbeque trout. You'll have to try it some time."

"Does she add spices?" Barsotti grabbed another handful of paperwork.

"A few. Like thyme and rosemary."

"Chili?"

"A bit, I think."

"Garlic?"

"No."

"Really? Everyone loves garlic."

"Shrike doesn't."

He tossed the paperwork back into the glove box and closed it. "Huh. So why does she carry it in her bag? An officer noticed it when getting her stuff out of the shower stall."

Lark realized that she had wandered into a minefield. *Does he know where she got that garlic necklace from?* The question sat heavy in the back of her mind. She smiled bashfully.

"That was me. We used to pull little pranks on each other when we were kids and, I don't know. I was feeling nostalgic or something."

Barsotti studied her for a moment. "Really?"

"Yeah."

He rolled his eyes and opened the latch to get to the back seat.

"We've explained the blood," Wren said. "So, what probable cause do you still have, officer?"

"Well, there are those two murders—"

"Two?" Lark asked.

"Joe Rose and Luke Young."

Shrike pulled away from Wren. "You're accusing us of hurting our father?"

Wren jumped in front of her, blocking her off from Barsotti.

"That's a hell of a temper you have there," Barsotti said.

"I would never hurt my family."

Barsotti arched an eyebrow. "But other people are fair game?"

"You have Lisa," Wren said. "She confessed."

"I don't know if you've noticed, but she's not quite right in the head. Makes me wonder. How could a woman like that track you down? According to your credit card receipts, you guys travel like you're throwing darts at a map. It would be hard to predict what state you're in, let alone the city. But somehow, a woman with no resources and only a tenuous grip on reality managed to find your exact hotel."

"She has moments of lucidity," Wren said.

"Oh," Barsotti said and continued rummaging through the truck. "Well, that explains everything. Case closed."

"The case *is* closed," Wren said. "Lisa is ill. She killed our father and she's now getting the help she needs."

Barsotti pulled Lark's backpack closer. "That's a unique response. Most people want everyone involved in the murder of their loved ones caught."

"You know that from experience?" Shrike taunted.

"We'll talk to the detective in charge of the case," Wren said. "Thank you for your interest. But I think you're seeing things that aren't there."

Barsotti twitched. "Have all of you forgotten that I was in the room when you talked to Lisa? I heard what she said to you."

"You were there? That whole day is a blur." Lark shivered, hugged herself, and lowered her gaze. She had perfected her lost little girl act. "What did she say?"

Again, Barsotti watched her for a heartbeat before responding. "You have to undo what you did. We were supposed to die. You have to kill us all."

She frowned and looked to her siblings. "I don't understand. What was she talking about?"

"I have no idea," Wren said.

Shrike didn't take her eyes off Barsotti as she shrugged.

"Wow, that's convincing," Barsotti dismissed.

Shrike took another step toward him. Wren shoved her back.

"Officer Barsotti," Wren said curtly. "If all you have are the ravings of a mad woman—"

"She had been medicated for a few days when you saw her," Barsotti interrupted. "Again, it makes you wonder. How did she track you down all on her lonesome?"

Wren stiffened. "You have no reason to search our property. We'd like to leave now."

"What did you have against Luke Young?" Barsotti asked.

"We don't know who that is," Lark said.

"You know for a fact that neither of your siblings knew him? Don't want to take a second and ask?" He gestured to Shrike and Wren.

Lark's brow furrowed. "They're my siblings."

"So, you know everyone they know?"

"Yeah." Lark laughed. "That's how siblings work."

"It's really not." He spoke to Lark but kept his eyes on Shrike. "You three seem oddly close. Almost disturbingly so. And it's weird how much they baby you. Do you realize you're an adult?"

Wren threw an elbow into Shrike's stomach to keep her from responding.

"Your siblings were caught fighting outside of Luke Young's murder scene."

"I thought you straightened that out," Lark said innocently. "It was all a misunderstanding."

"Shrike was caught on the store's camera."

"You didn't see my face," Shrike blurted out.

Wren cleared his throat, and Shrike realized what she had just said.

Suppressing her anger, she added, "Because I wasn't there."

Barsotti laughed. "Convincing."

"Just because she's not good at expressing herself doesn't mean that she's lying," Wren said calmly. "She wasn't caught on camera because she was never in the store. It must have been someone else."

Barsotti leaned against the side of the truck. "Another six-foot-three blonde woman who's built like a linebacker and has that exact same jacket?"

"It's possible," Wren said.

"Maybe it was a man," Lark added. "It's hard to tell in winter gear."

Barsotti watched Shrike like he was waiting for her to snap. "You know what caught my attention? The woman on the tape bought a necklace of garlic bulbs. Exactly like the one you have in your bag."

"That was me, remember?" Lark said. "I put them there."

"Of course, you did," Barsotti said.

Shrike clenched her jaw and her face flushed red.

"Why were you going to an occult shop, Shrike?" Barsotti asked. "You don't seem like the spiritual type."

Shrike glanced to Lark.

"She—"

"I asked Shrike," Barsotti said. "I'm sure she's capable of answering on her own."

"I wasn't there."

"I'm getting real sick of being lied to," Barsotti replied.

"We don't have to talk to you," Wren said. "We're going to leave now."

Barsotti's eyes narrowed. "No one heard your dad scream. Forensics found no evidence that he had been gagged and given the state of the room, he went down hard."

"Why are you telling us this?" Lark whimpered.

"Lisa followed him around the room, stabbing him over and over."

"Stop," Wren snapped.

"How did no one hear that? Everyone heard you lot screaming, but no one heard him fighting for his life? Does that make sense to you?"

Tears pricked the back of Lark's eyes and her throat swelled shut.

"We're in mourning," Wren said. "How dare you—"

"I tried playing nice. Whatever killed Joe is still out there and it's going to kill again. You know it. I know it. Stop stonewalling me."

"We don't know anything!" Lark pleaded.

He slammed his fist against the truck's roof. Lark flinched back with a yelp. It was a small sound that sent Shrike rushing forward. It took both Wren and Lark to keep her from hitting the officer.

"Shrike! Don't!" Lark said.

Shrike growled. "Stay away from my sister."

"This is your reaction to her being startled and I'm supposed to believe you're not capable of murder?" Barsotti said. "Is that why you helped Lisa kill Joe? Did daddy dearest scare the baby?"

Shrike surged forward, driving both of her siblings back.

"It's a trap!" Wren shouted. "He's got nothing on us, Shrike. That's why he's trying to get you to hit him."

Lark pushed against Shrike with everything she had. "Still breathing?"

Shrike jerked to a stop. Keeping his weight against Shrike, Wren placed a hand on his chest and took a noisy exaggerated breath.

"Still breathing," he confirmed.

Lark mimicked him. "Still breathing."

None of them moved for a tense moment. Then Shrike thumped a hand against her chest. Pressed against her, Lark felt her sister tremble, heard the air rush into her lungs and her heart pound.

"Still breathing," Shrike whispered.

The tension slowly ebbed from her body.

"That was weird," Barsotti commented.

Lark whipped around to face him. "When did you get so cruel?"

"When you gave me no other option." Barsotti ran a hand over his face. "You claimed Joe's remains. That really puts me under a time crunch."

"Wait. How do you know we have Dad?" Wren asked.

"I told them to contact me when they released him."

Wren shook his head. "Why?"

"Because he was the only thing keeping you here. Once you had him, you were going to run."

"We collected him hours ago," Lark said. "We could have left by now but we're still here. I don't know why you think so badly of us, but you're clearly wrong."

Barsotti scrubbed his stubbled cheek. "Lisa had no history of mental illness. No criminal record. By all accounts, she was a normal woman living her life. Days after meeting the Rose family, she vanished. This girl left everything behind just to track down Joe. A task she was not mentally fit to accomplish. But she does it. And then she kills Joe in a way that seems almost physically impossible for her to pull off."

"Look—"

"I'm not done, Wren," Barsotti said. "Lisa commands you lot to kill. Barely a day later, Luke Young, a man I can connect two out of the three of you to, is brutally murdered in an eerily similar fashion to Joe. And all the while, you've been bouncing around the city, constantly changing motels, and acting erratically. All of that caught on camera. Now you show up again to fight Robby."

"He attacked Lark," Shrike snapped.

"That's all coincidence," Lark insisted.

Barsotti stepped closer to her, ignoring Shrike's warning glare.

"Lark," he said softly. "I was the first one on the scene. I took a pummeling from Shrike and held you as you cried. I arranged for you to see Lisa and protected you when things went bad. I'm not a stranger to you. Don't lie to me."

She tried to look away, but he caught her gaze.

"I'm standing right here, ready and willing to protect you again. Just talk to me."

"Leave her alone," Wren said.

"Lark's not a child," Barsotti said before refocusing on her. "Come on, Lark. Let me help you. Tell me what you saw."

"I don't remember."

"You don't just forget the things we saw," Barsotti whispered. "I know you want to talk to me. It's killing you to keep it inside."

Lark wiped away a tear and shook her head.

"All right. We'll do it the hard way." Barsotti sighed. "Get in my cruiser."

"What?" Lark squeaked.

"I'm arresting you."

"On what charge?" Wren demanded.

"Credit card fraud. Lark's checked into three hotels using Joe's card."

"But, he was our dad," Lark stammered as Barsotti pulled his handcuffs from his belt and thumbed them open. "He always let me use it."

"The estate hasn't been settled and none of you have contacted the credit card company about his death."

"It's a family account," Wren said.

"So you say."

Wren motioned for Shrike to keep back. "I've handled the finances since I was eighteen. I know for a fact that we have a legal right to use that account. One call to the bank will clear this all up."

Barsotti shrugged. "You can borrow my phone when we get to the station."

"This is all just to make sure we don't leave."

"Oh, Wren, you're the brains of the operation, aren't you?"

Wren flushed. "You can't do this."

"File a complaint at the station. Oh, and I'm impounding the truck. All that blood splatter has me suspicious. You guys want a lift?" Barsotti jingled the cuffs in front of Lark's face. "Wrists up."

"Can I have my bag?" Lark asked.

"No."

"Please."

"There could be weapons in it. You're not trustworthy." Barsotti glanced at Shrike, silently challenging her to make a move.

"Barsotti, please. I just want Dad's ashes."

He snapped back around to Lark, his smirk fading. "Joe's in here?"

"I want my dad," she sniffed.

Barsotti gently opened the backpack and pulled the box out. Without a word, he held it out for her to take.

"Thank you." Clutching it, her vision blurring with tears, she barely felt the cool metal encircling her wrists.

"We don't have to do this," Barsotti said. "We can go back inside, have a cup of coffee, and just talk."

"We've told you every way we could," Wren said. "We don't know anything."

"Suit yourself," Barsotti said and tightened the handcuffs.

# Chapter 10

Wren clutched his laptop to his chest, his eyes locked on the city streets that passed by the windows. He barely dared to breathe on the off chance that Barsotti would take it as a challenge. The officer had eyed his laptop with clear interest when he had taken it from the truck, but he hadn't asked about it. The restraint was unnerving. Wren had always thought he was a good judge of character. Not as skilled as Lark, but good enough to get the general idea of a man. This sudden shift in Barsotti had blindsided him. Wren had underestimated not just how far the officer was willing to go, but how competent he was. He had judged Barsotti as a man who didn't care enough about his job to be particularly good at it. Passably competent, at best. This sudden aggressive persistence had caught Wren off guard. And the connections Barsotti had already made were unnerving. Wren turned to study the man behind the wheel, trying to figure out what else he knew. Barsotti hadn't said a word since they had piled into the cruiser. It was possible he had laid all his cards on the table. It was just as likely that he knew a lot more than he was saying.

Tightening his arms around his laptop, Wren glanced at his sisters. Barsotti had insisted that Shrike ride in the back of the police cruiser with the still-handcuffed Lark. They were both deathly silent. Lark had the box of ashes on her lap and had dented the corners with her constant fussing. She had wiggled against her seat belt so she could snuggle under Shrike's arm. Shrike absently stroked her little sister's hair. A soft gesture that seemed to soothe them both. Wren wished he was back there with them, even if that was on the wrong side of the divider.

"Can you move this up a bit? There's barely any room back here,"

Shrike grumbled and smacked her knee into the divider.

"No," Barsotti replied.

"My legs are cramping."

"I can't do anything about that. Even if I could, a responsible driver doesn't mess with their seat settings while the vehicle is in motion," Barsotti replied.

Shrike snorted. "Yeah, you're real responsible."

"My job is trying to prevent people from killing themselves and others through acts of sheer stupidity," he deadpanned. "It would be hypocritical not to follow through myself."

She kicked the divider sharply.

Barsotti glanced at her in the rearview mirror. "And here I thought you would have had a bit more respect for road rules, given your history."

Wren's stomach dropped when Shrike's shoulders bunched.

"My history?" Shrike demanded.

"Your mother died in a car crash, right? Head-on collision with your grandparents. All three killed on impact."

"You son of—"

"Shrike," Wren cut in.

Capturing her gaze, he shook his head. She slowly released a breath between her clenched teeth. Her face was bright red and her shoulders were tense, but she kept quiet.

Wren turned to Barsotti. "Stop trying to provoke her."

"I'm just making conversation," Barsotti said innocently.

Wren tightened his grip on his laptop. Shrike had always been an easy target. Her temper made her stupid and it wasn't a surprise that Barsotti had figured that out. Wren was worried how far the officer would take it.

"Why are you acting like this?" Wren asked.

"I'm just doing my job."

"Something happened to you. Something's changed," Wren said.

Barsotti shot him a quick glance. "Tell me your secrets and I'll tell you mine."

*How much do you know?* Wren bit his lips and looked out his window.

"That's what I thought," Barsotti muttered.

They turned off the highway and entered the empty city streets.

Barsotti broke the silence again. "So, you cremated Joe, huh?"

"What about it?" Shrike asked.

Wren cleared his throat. She glared at him and ground her teeth but managed to keep quiet.

"I'm just a little hurt that I wasn't invited to the service," Barsotti said.

"You didn't know him," Shrike snapped.

"Shrike," Wren whispered sharply. "Please."

After a second, Shrike kissed the top of Lark's head and tried to calm down.

"Granted, I didn't see him alive. But he did earn me a few hours of mandated therapy," Barsotti said. He met Wren's questioning gaze for a brief second. "Seeing a continuous rotation of corpses can wear a person down."

"You're a traffic cop," Wren said.

"Accidents happen. And those accidents can spread out over a surprisingly large stretch of highway." Barsotti diligently checked all the mirrors as he slowed the car for a red light.

A bus rambled through the intersection. Wren tensed. He was too slow to see who was behind the wheel. He pried one hand off his laptop and pressed it to his chest. His heart was beating so hard it felt like his palm would bruise.

"Still breathing," he whispered.

Lark whimpered and picked at the edge of the box. "Still breathing."

"Still breathing," Shrike pushed out through clenched teeth.

"Okay, I'm going to need someone to explain what the hell that's all about," Barsotti asked.

Wren jumped on the chance to distract him from Shrike.

"It's something our dad taught us," Wren said. "A way to remind us to stop and take perspective."

"Joe taught you guys a lot?"

"Of course," Wren said. "That's what fathers do."

Barsotti grunted. "What kind of man was Joe?"

Shrike answered instantly, "Better than you. Better than anyone."

"It's a shame you didn't get to talk to him," Lark mumbled. "He would have made you a nicer person."

Barsotti glanced to Wren. "And what do you think?"

"The world doesn't make sense without him," Wren said.

Barsotti whistled, the light changed, and he inched them through the intersection. "Wow. Seems like a hell of a guy. And yet you had no one to call."

"What do you mean?" Wren asked.

"For the funeral. You'd think a man as great as Joe would have hundreds of people vying to get to his service. But it was just you guys. Seems odd."

"How did you know that?" Wren demanded an instant before he realized something. "They told you when you called about the remains."

"We might have had a chat," Barsotti said.

Wren glared at him. "Don't you feel any guilt talking to us like this? We're in pain."

"What if it was your dad who died?" Lark asked softly.

Barsotti laughed before he could stop himself.

"You don't get along with your dad?" Lark asked.

"It's complicated," Barsotti dismissed. "So why didn't you invite any of Joe's friends?"

The siblings looked at each other. None of them answered.

"No friends, huh?"

Wren released a slow breath. "None that could make the trip."

"No other family?"

"No," Wren said.

"What about you guys?" Barsotti asked. "I know that none of you are legally married, but what about boyfriends? Girlfriends? Not one of you had someone to call for a bit of support?"

Wren licked his lips and repeated, "None that could make the trip."

Barsotti contemplated that for a moment. "No."

"What?" Wren asked.

"I'm not buying it. I think it's been just the four of you for a very long time. Long enough that all of you could die tomorrow and no one would notice."

Blindsided by the truth, Wren felt like the earth had dropped out from under him. It hadn't even occurred to him to inform anyone about his father's death. Even now, he couldn't think of anyone he would bother to tell. Barsotti's words sunk into his mind, and he tried to prove them wrong. All he needed was one person that would care if they weren't around. One person that would miss them. Just one single person that would think about them when they were gone. His mind was blank. It occurred to him then that if they died trying to stop Trent, no one would even come to claim their bodies. They would be left on the slab or in a freezer somewhere then cremated to make room for other nameless corpses.

"Oh, God, I was just trying to provoke a reaction. Am I right?" Barsotti asked. "Are you really that isolated?"

*We'll rot with no one to care,* Wren realized. He twisted around to look at his sisters. Lark had paled and her hands shook as she clutched the box to her chest. Shrike met his gaze but said nothing.

"Where do you think we'll go when we die?" Lark whispered. "Do you think we'll get to be together? Do you think we'll see Dad again?"

Barsotti glanced back at them as they entered an intersection. Wren glimpsed movement behind the officer.

"Look out!" Wren shouted.

Barsotti looked back, spotted the bus that had run the red light, and slammed on the brakes.

***

Shrike threw herself on Lark as the police cruiser spun out. The air stank of burning tires. The car jerked to a stop. Shrike's seat belt pulled tight, crushing the air from her lungs. Shrike braced for the pain, but it didn't come. The engine clicked a few times then the night fell silent.

"Wren?" Shrike asked.

"I'm okay. Are you guys all right?"

"Fine," Lark said.

Slowly, Shrike unfurled from around her sister.

"We crushed him," Lark whispered. Her slender hands fluttered over the crumpled edges of the box. "I'm sorry, Dad. We didn't mean to."

Anger flared inside Shrike, and she slammed her hand against the metal grating.

"What the hell was that, Barsotti? So much for being a good driver."

He didn't respond. He clutched the emergency brake with one hand while the other still gripped the wheel. Shrike followed his gaze. The bus that had run the red light had careened across the street and jumped the curb. It stopped a few inches short of crashing into a brick building. Nothing moved inside the bus. The city street was empty.

"They swerved to hit us," Wren said.

"Maybe the driver just had a stroke or something," Lark said, her fingers tightening around the box.

Barsotti stiffly released his grip and unclicked his seat belt. "Wren, you're getting in the back."

"What? Why?"

"Because I need to check on this and I don't trust you," Barsotti said.

Lark grabbed Shrike's hand.

"He can't go alone," she whispered. "What if it's Trent?"

Grinding her teeth, Shrike smacked the grating again. "I'm coming with you."

Barsotti snorted. "What are you going to do if someone's hurt? Carry them off the bus yourself?"

"I'm actually capable of that. Scared people do stupid things. You're going to need someone to watch your back," Shrike insisted.

Barsotti rubbed his hands through his hair and jumped his shoulders. "Fine. But Wren and Lark stay here."

Shrike agreed before either of her siblings could argue. Undoing her seat belt, she kissed Lark's forehead and assured her that everything was fine. Wren fumbled with his seat belt, but Barsotti grabbed his arm. He hadn't looked away from the bus.

"Stay up front."

"I thought you wanted me in the back?"

"I do," Barsotti said. He scrubbed his face until his nails left marks. "There's a firehouse nearby. Two blocks down and one to the right. Got it?"

"No," Wren said. "I'm not following you at all."

"Two blocks down, one to the right," Lark repeated.

"Yeah." Barsotti dropped his hands. He barely looked in Wren's direction. His focus was on the bus. "Anything goes wrong, let your sister out and follow her. Don't look back. Just keep running."

Wren's brow furrowed. "What do you think is going to go wrong?"

Barsotti took a deep breath and looked at each sibling in turn. He got out of the car without responding.

Shrike waited for the door to close behind him before hurriedly whispering, "How much does he know?"

Wren and Lark both shrugged. They flinched when Barsotti opened the back door.

"Shrike?" Lark asked.

"I'll be okay," she added in a lower voice. "I'll catch up."

Barsotti closed the door the moment she was out of the way. His deep breath churned to mist in the still morning air.

"Stay behind me," he said.

Their footsteps echoed down the empty street. It was quiet enough to hear the click of the traffic lights changing. Barsotti kept a slow, steady pace. Halfway through the intersection, he stopped.

"What is it?" Shrike asked.

"You don't feel that?" He pulled his sidearm and flicked the safety off.

A chill ran down her spine and left her shivering. She swallowed thickly and tried to sound casual.

"What exactly am I supposed to be feeling?"

"I can't tell if you're really that oblivious," he said.

He started forward again, silent and slow. Shrike glanced back to Wren and Lark. They would know how to ask all the questions that were jumbled up in her head.

"Don't you have any survival instincts, Shrike?"

"I don't know what you're talking about."

He paused, looked over his shoulder, and held her gaze. "Yes, you do."

Shrike forced herself to shrug. She was too tense. The motion was stiff and unnatural. "No."

Barsotti fumbled with his duty belt. He pulled a small cylinder free—an expandable baton that he opened with a flick of his wrist.

"You don't want this then?"

"You're giving me a weapon?"

He flipped the baton around in his palm and offered her the handle. She took it.

"You're afraid," she commented.

"Sometimes, that twist in your gut is the only warning sign you get. You want to live? Trust your instincts. Your other senses will lie to you. Your instincts never will."

Shrike nodded and readjusted her grip on the baton. Images of Trent flashed through her mind's eye. The baton suddenly felt thin and fragile. It seemed laughable to go up against something like Trent with a stick.

"We okay?" Barsotti asked. "This is my responsibility, not yours. I can take you back to the cruiser."

Shrike eyed the bus. Nothing moved inside of it. There was no noise. But that didn't mean they were alone. Robby had alluded to the homeless going missing. If Trent was picking them off during his late-night shifts, it was possible that there were still living victims inside the bus. She couldn't stomach just walking away.

She squared her shoulders and cracked her neck. "We're good."

Barsotti nodded once, cradled his gun between both hands, and started for the bus door. Shrike followed a step behind. They crossed the intersection and jumped onto the curb. Barsotti took the lead. He moved with controlled focus and crouched low, constantly scanning the area. They slowed their pace as they walked along the length of the bus. The suspension squeaked as something thudded against the metal siding. Shrike jumped back. Barsotti spun around, lifting his gun on reflex. Their breathing and the click of the changing traffic lights broke the silence. Barsotti turned to her. It took her a second to realize that he was looking for reassurance. He wasn't sure that she had heard it too. Shrike nodded. The confirmation seemed to steady him. For a moment, she felt guilty for stonewalling him. If he had seen the living shadows, if he knew that there was something unnatural hiding in the dark, they were leaving him to face it on his own. At least she had Wren and Lark. She had two people to remind her that she wasn't insane.

Barsotti tipped his head toward the door. She nodded and fell into step behind him again. As they crept closer, she realized that the folding door was open. It made her hesitate. Barsotti pushed out a long breath, his air churning into fog before him. Carefully, he dipped and took a quick glance inside. Standing back up, he caught her gaze. He shook his head. Shrike frowned.

*What?* she mouthed.

Sighing, he took one hand off his gun and created an 'O' with his fingers and thumb. *He didn't see anyone,* she realized. Awkwardly, she gave him a thumbs-up. It was never this difficult with family. Barsotti slipped up the small flight of stairs with impressive stealth. He kept low, using the railing for cover, and peeked into the aisle. Shrike waited. It was weird not being the one to lead the charge. Finally, Barsotti straightened and motioned for her to follow. She bounced up the stairs. The air inside the bus was so cold it hurt. Barsotti kept his gun high as he headed down the aisle. He made it to the back and turned around, his brow furrowed.

"No one's here," he mumbled.

"Okay."

"Okay? Shrike, I kept my eyes on the bus. Barely looked away for a second. There's no way anyone left without me seeing them."

"So what are you saying? Someone rigged the bus to keep going and jumped out?"

She cringed at how feeble the excuse sounded and avoided his gaze. Turning to the driver's seat, she studied the dashboard and pedals, hoping to find something that might explain it all away. Nothing looked out of place. Barsotti came up behind her. She felt the heat of his body before she heard him. Realization hit her like a physical blow. This could be a trap set up by the demon. Barsotti brought them here. He separated her from her siblings. He lured her onto the bus with just a stick to protect herself. Her eyes flicked between his gun and his haggard face. *What if he is working with the demon? Is that why he keeps hinting about it? Is that how he knows so much? Is that why he's suddenly acting so different?* Each thought made it a little harder to breathe.

"How did the bus keep going?" he mumbled.

A shadow raced across the windshield. She flinched back and smacked into him.

"What is it?" Barsotti asked.

*He brought me here,* a voice in her head screamed.

"Hey, are you okay?"

*Is he possessed?*

"Shrike?"

She stared at his hands. His thumb restlessly stroked the side of his gun.

"We need to leave," she said. "This is wrong."

"Yeah." Barsotti stepped back and motioned for her to head out first.

She took a step and paused. Metal crashed against metal. They both turned to the back of the bus. The roof's emergency hatch was now open. The bus had grown dark enough that the invading shaft of light looked almost solid. Fat snowflakes drifted inside. Everything was still. Barsotti and Shrike shared a glance before raising their eyes to the ceiling. Metal squealed and buckled. Something scraped across the top of the bus. The moment they focused on it, the folding door snapped shut. Barsotti jumped down the few stairs and yanked on the door. It wouldn't open. He pulled on the emergency release, but it didn't do any good. Looking back at her, he motioned to the control panel. Scanning the collection of buttons and levers, she found the release and flipped it. Barsotti pulled on the door. It still didn't open.

The temperature plummeted. Frost spread out over the windows, coating them, and blotting out the light. A shadow streaked across one side of the bus and slammed against the door. Barsotti staggered back. Grabbing the back of his shirt, she yanked him up the last of the stairs and kept him on his feet. The roof buckled as something struck against it. Before they could cringe back, the blur returned, passing by the opposite side of the bus.

Barsotti kept his gun up with one arm and shoved her behind him with the other. The shadow raced across the windshield, scraping against the glass, and creating a shrill sound. Before they could turn, something struck the roof again. This time, it was a rhythmic pounding. Like something huge was stalking across the top of the bus. It was heading for the open hatch. Barsotti cursed under his breath and aimed at the hole.

"There's the emergency exit at the back." Shrike pushed him. "Go."

Barsotti bit his lip. The footsteps had almost reached the opening. They could be running right to it.

"Police! Stop, or I'll shoot!"

"That's not going to work." Shrike shoved him again, trying to get him to move.

The bus rattled with every step.

"Just covering my bases," he muttered.

Darkness blotted out the light and falling snow. Claws scraped at the opening. Barsotti fired three times in rapid succession. Shrike wasn't prepared for how loud it was. The walls amplified the thunderous cracks until her ears rang. She barely heard Barsotti when he ordered her to move. Keeping the gun trained on the hatch, he stepped between the seats, giving her enough room to pass.

"Go, Shrike!"

Ears still squealing, she sprinted down the row. Shadows swirled and pressed against the frosted-over glass. She didn't want to go out there. But the thought that Wren and Lark were on their own in this chaos propelled her forward. *We told them to run. They'll be at the fire station. They're okay.* She repeated the promises to herself, grabbed the release, and lifted the baton high.

"Barsotti?"

She glanced back. The unseen creature slammed against the roof. The windows cracked and the bus rocked, almost throwing her off her feet. Barsotti bounced off the edges of the seats as he sprinted toward her. Shadows crept around the edges of the hatch in thick tendrils. Rapidly-forming claws scraped at the roof until the metal buckled.

"Go!" Barsotti screamed.

Shrike yanked on the handle. Frost had coated the hinges. She pushed again and the thin ice cracked, but the door still wouldn't open. Barsotti reached her. Shrike tossed him the baton, grabbed the latch with both hands, and strained until her arms ached. The ice shattered and the latch jerked up. The bus rocked as the creature on the roof tried to get inside. Shrike rammed her shoulder against the door until it snapped open, and she toppled out onto the road. The morning light was blinding. Snow fell around her but after the bitter cold, she began to sweat. Barsotti jumped down as she pushed up onto all fours. He dropped the baton beside her and rested a hand between her shoulder blades. The touch was gentle, but his fingertips brushed the edges of her bite mark. She hissed and flinched away.

"Are you okay?" Barsotti asked. "Are you hurt?"

She smacked his hand away, grabbed the baton, and jumped to her feet. "Where is it?"

"I don't know."

Looking back through the open emergency door, she found the bus brightly lit and intact. No frost. No darkness. No twisted metal. Panting, they each turned around. The street was empty and still. It was snowing hard now. Plump snowflakes that quickly coated them both. Shrike peered through the storm to see the police cruiser. Lark now sat up front with Wren. She leaned against the steering wheel and raised her cuffed hands in a silent demand for answers. Wren mirrored the same puzzled, questioning motion. Shrike shook her head and started back toward them. Barsotti kept pace beside her, having to slightly jog to keep up with her longer stride.

"Both of you, get in the back," he ordered when he saw them.

Wren and Lark looked at Shrike.

"Now!" Barsotti snapped.

Shrike nodded. Scrambling to obey, they left the front doors open for them to jump in quickly. Barsotti and Shrike both locked the doors the moment they were inside.

"What happened?" Wren asked.

"Did you hear anything?" Barsotti demanded.

"No," Shrike said.

"Not you. Them. Lark, Wren, did you hear anything when we were in the bus?"

"Like what?" Lark asked.

Still catching his breath, Barsotti checked his gun and smacked his head back against the seat.

"You didn't hear anything out of the ordinary?" he pressed.

Wren leaned against the divider. "No. You went in. Everything was quiet. A few minutes passed and you came running out the back."

"Barsotti, are you okay?" Lark asked.

"I'm three bullets down." He trembled as he twisted around. "I fired three shots. How did you not hear that? How did you not see the shadows?"

Lark and Wren flinched back. Shrike grabbed Barsotti's wrist and forced it down against the dash. It didn't seem like he even realized he was brandishing the gun. Barsotti kept his eyes on her as his breathing evened out.

"You saw it," he said.

Shrike clenched her jaw, uncertain how to answer. She couldn't risk becoming his star witness. But he was close to losing it, and one more lie could drive him over the edge. She didn't know what he was capable of. She didn't trust him. His hand shook so hard that the gun barrel tapped against the dash.

"Let it go," she said.

He released the gun and pushed it further away with his fingertips. Shrike kept her grip.

"You saw it," he repeated.

She bit her lip.

"Damn it, Shrike! Just admit it. Just once."

*Of course, I saw,* she thought. *And that was the whole point.* Trent wanted them to know how helpless they really were. It wasn't just that there was no one waiting for them to come home. Or that there was no one to come looking for them if they went missing. Trent wanted them to know that no one was going to help them. No one could. She had been turned away from all the religious houses she had visited. The occult shop owner, the one person who said they could help, had died a fraud. And the police weren't even a deterrent. Maybe it had Barsotti, maybe not. Either way, it wasn't afraid to show itself in front of him. It had Barsotti so twisted up that Shrike didn't feel safe around him. Trent had proved his point. They were utterly alone. Shrike released his wrist and slumped into the passenger seat.

Barsotti stared at her with a look of betrayal and fear. "It wasn't just in my head. It wasn't. I…"

He looked to each of the siblings, but they all kept silent and avoided his gaze.

"I know what I saw," he whispered.

Not knowing what else to do, Barsotti numbly put on his seat belt, turned on the engine, and slowly pulled back out onto the street.

# Chapter 11

Lark steadied herself as the subway train charged through the underground tunnel. The concrete walls amplified the sounds of the wheels grinding against the tracks. She moved aimlessly through the carriages, accustomed to the random bumps and sways. The midnight train was more popular than she had anticipated. Ruckus Robbie had been right. The homeless weren't turning to buses to escape the bitter cold. They had come here. She passed huddled groups and realized quickly that they were sleeping in shifts. Each group had at least one person awake. She could feel them watching her. Their fear was palpable.

The train lurched around the final corner, and they started a slight descent into the depot station. Lark gripped a safety rail, hugging it tightly as the overhead lights flickered. All around her, the lookouts straightened and squirmed, searching every corner of the carriage. They were as fearful of the shadows as she was. The tunnel lights dimmed, and the windows became black mirrors. Swallowing down a whimper, Lark pulled her phone out of her jacket pocket. There wasn't any reception underground, but it was still comforting to hold it. Like a lifeline to her siblings.

Puffing out her cheeks, she squirmed out of her backpack and hugged it to her chest. Her breath caught when the contents shifted. *Where's Dad?* Panic had her fumbling with the zipper before she remembered that they had hidden him away. That had been the moment when the notion that they could die became a stark reality. It had gutted her to bury him under some random tree off the interstate. But there was no one else to keep him and she'd be damned if she risked her father's ashes ending up in a gutter. The tree was better. He'd be safe there until whoever survived could go back for him. Wren had accounted for it in all his contingency plans. And if none of them made it out, at least their dad would be laid to rest somewhere kind of pretty.

She tightened her grip on her bag, feeling the chafer fuel containers clatter about. They had been her suggestion. Trailer parks weren't popular in the winter, so Shrike and Lark would pick up shifts at the local ski lodge. Shrike was a guide and ski instructor, Lark a waitress. The containers of ethanol gel they used to warm the breakfast buffets burned surprisingly hot. They lighted easily and it had always looked sticky to her. Plan A was to make sure it ended up on Trent.

Sucking in a deep breath, she glanced around at the carriage. People became restless as they neared the depot. A few of the lookouts shook their friends awake. There were hushed conversations and darting glances. Lark's stomach dropped when they started to crowd under the brighter overhead lights, each one hunching down so they couldn't be seen from the outside. The midnight train wouldn't stay here long. A few moments and it would set off around the city again. Still, people prepared.

Lark hugged her bag and gripped her phone as the train slowed. They crept through the last few yards of the dimly lit tunnel. The overhead lights sputtered, allowing weak shadows to gather under the seats. They seemed to squirm in the corner of her eyes. But when she looked at them directly, they were just shadows. She tightened her grip on the safety bar.

The speakers crackled, and an automated voice announced that they had reached the depot station. An instant later, the brakes engaged and, with a squeal of metal on metal, they slipped out of the tunnel. The underground station was cavernous. Hundreds of stark white neon lights made the place so bright Lark winced. There was only a handful of people waiting on the platform. The train rattled to a final stop, and the doors opened with a hiss. Cold air rushed into the carriage. Lark shivered violently and zipped her coat up to her neck. No one was quick to leave. The few people on the platform rushed forward, hugging themselves for warmth. The heavy footsteps woke one of the sleeping men. He groggily stood, gave a full body shiver, and stumbled toward the exit. A woman darted forward and grabbed his arm.

"Are you crazy?" She demanded.

The man blinked a few times. "They let us stay here."

"No one stays here anymore," she said.

"What are you talking about?" He feebly tried to pull himself free of her grip. "The cops don't move us from the depot."

"It's not the cops you need to worry about," someone called from the far end of the carriage. "Stay onboard, you moron."

The people who had just entered the carriage shot uncomfortable glances at each other. Now that she was looking for it, Lark noticed a dozen people having similar conversations. Many people had cowered a little further back from the doors. But there were a few that had pressed closer to the windows, searching for something among the pillars and scattered benches.

"The heater's clearly malfunctioning," the woman said, desperate to keep the man from leaving. "It's warmer here."

The man was still considering this when the speakers announced that the train was about to leave. The sharp ding that followed snapped Lark back to her senses. She had been too fixated on the conversations around her. Darting forward, she barely got through the doors before they closed.

"Get back in here, stupid girl!"

Lark stumbled onto the platform and turned to see who had spoken. It was the same woman who had stopped the man. She gaped at Lark as the doors slid shut. A few others were looking at Lark too, their expressions ranging from concern to complete disinterest. There was a gush of air as the train began to move again, heading back toward the tunnel. Seeing the fear in the stranger's eyes stripped Lark of her bravery. She watched the train go, curling around her bag and squeezing her phone. The train sunk into the flickering lights of the tunnel. The sound lingered for a few minutes. Then it was gone, and her ears rung with the utter silence. Lark slowly spun around. Her shoes squeaked against the floor tiles. The platform was deserted. She had thought that at least a handful of people would have gotten off to catch a connecting bus. Shivering, she waited, half certain that a late-night cleaner or security guard would pass by.

No one came.

A chill swept up her spine, and she gasped. The bare walls echoed the sound. Footsteps rushed behind her. Lark choked on a squeal and whipped around. No one was there. The overhead lights kept the shadows dim. Pillars broke up the far side of the platform, creating a dozen hiding places. Something shuffled. Holding her breath, she strained to make sense of the distant muffled noise. It could have been whispered voices. It could have just been the blood rushing through her ears. With the echo, she couldn't even tell where it was coming from.

Backing up, she glanced at her phone screen. Still no reception. She contemplated faking a call. It was something her dad had taught them when they were younger. *If you feel threatened, pretend you're not alone. It'll make them second-guess attacking you.* The memory almost made her laugh. She doubted that trick would work with a demon. *You're the bait,* she reminded herself. *You're supposed to be afraid. You're supposed to be a target.* Lark forced herself to move again. She backed up a few steps, turned around, and started for the elevators at a quick pace. Her skin prickled, and her gut rolled. It wasn't the same as she had felt before. She didn't feel a predator breathing down her neck. It was more like its presence had tainted the air. Lark felt like she had stepped into the demon's nest.

The shuffling sound returned. Without breaking stride, she glanced over her shoulder. The platform was still empty. Forcing herself not to run, Lark fixed her eyes on the elevator doors before her. The temperature dropped with every step. It had her teeth chattering. Skidding to a stop, she hit the call button and glanced behind. Light reflected off the tiles and made her eyes ache. A soft thud echoed off the walls. She hit the call button again. Movement drew her eyes to the left.

A narrow guard's booth was tucked beside the elevator. Condensation frosted its windows. A dark shape surged toward the glass. The sliding door flew open, and Lark jumped back with a squeal.

A bored-looking guard leaned through the gap. "It's broken."

"What?" She panted.

"The elevator. It keeps acting up. You'll have to take the stairs."

"Oh." Lark smiled. "Thank you."

The guard looked her over. "You don't need me to walk you out, do you?"

"No, that's not necessary."

"There's a few more folks waiting for the last bus, so there's no reason to work yourself up. You're as safe as you ever were."

She wondered how scared she looked. "Thank you."

He threaded an arm through the gap to point out the right direction. "Just down that tunnel and up the stairs." The guard cursed and pulled his arm back into the booth. "Goddam heaters. I've had people out three times to fix the damn thing."

Still muttering under his breath, the guard closed the sliding window, trapping the heat that was fogging the glass. And just like that, she was alone again. Lark swallowed thickly and entered the tunnel at the end of the platform. Tattered posters were plastered over the walls. Voices echoed down the empty tunnel, telling her that there were still people waiting at the other end. As she walked, the sensation of being watched returned, stronger than it had been before. It was hard to tell if there was something unseen stalking behind her, or if it was just the cold, motionless eyes of the posters' stock images. Suddenly, their frozen smiles seemed cruel.

A row of exposed lights ran along the middle of the ceiling. There weren't any shadows. But there weren't any exits, either. Forward or back were her only options. Lark pressed a hand against her chest, took a deep breath, and picked up her pace. She tried to resist but couldn't keep herself from glancing behind. No one was there. She could still glimpse the guard's shadow moving over the frosted glass. A moment later, recorded sitcom laughter came from the booth. *At least we wouldn't have to worry about him interfering*, Lark thought. *Seems like he's settled in to watch his show.* The man wasn't going to leave the warmth of his booth unless he was forced out. There would be another guard watching over the bus lockup, but Shrike would handle that.

A gust of icy wind swept down the tunnel. It pushed her hair back and wrapped around her neck like a solid hand. Hunching her shoulders, she fumbled with her scarf, trying to keep the cold from slipping under her jacket. She almost missed the doors to the public toilets. Tattered posters camouflaged them with the wall. As subtly as she could, Lark glanced at the door handle. A barely visible slither of duct tape was stuck around the door edge. Her relieved sigh churned into mist before her. It would be her only sign that Shrike was here. It was a small promise that her sister had secured her another way out. The bathrooms had high-set windows that opened out into the depot. Normally, there was a metal grate to keep people out. Shrike would have broken the latch when she taped the bathroom locks open.

Lark took a steadying breath and studied the tunnel, looking for anything the demon might use against her if she had to lure it down here. There wasn't much. A trash bin at the entrance and a utility room she'd have to be careful to avoid. Lark eyed the distance between the mouth of the tunnel and the toilet door. It was further than she would have liked. Sprinting in winter gear was never easy, and she wasn't exactly fit to begin with. Reassuring herself that she could easily cover the distance, she endured another arctic blast. Her mittens were useless. Her fingers were numb by the time she reached the end of the tunnel.

Voices drifted down the long concrete staircase. Lark cautiously crept to the base of the stairs. With the slanted roof, she could only see their legs, but they looked human enough. Everyone was keeping close to the walls. Each gust of wind carried a fine dusting of snow deeper into the building.

"Still breathing," she whispered to herself.

Clutching her bag and phone to her chest, she jogged up the stairs. Something moved behind her, and she whipped around. A few of the tunnel's neon lights flickered, allowing shadows to strobe over the tunnel walls. Crouching to get a better look, she peered into the unstable light. A door slammed, and she lost her nerve. She ran up the last of the steps and joined the small group of people huddling for warmth. The air was so cold that it burned her lungs. A few people looked in her direction. They all quickly lost interest and returned to their conversations. Mostly, they were complaining about the broken heating system. Lark looked out the doors and her stomach dropped. Floodlights kept the outside world visible despite the heavy snowfall.

"It's really coming down," Lark said to no one in particular.

A man to her right rolled his eyes. "Oh yeah, I noticed that, too."

"Has it been like this for a while?" Lark asked.

The man shifted his weight. He was still irritated, but his voice softened a little.

"Nah, it just kicked up. They say the blizzard's going to hit in a few hours." He worked his jaw and glared out into the snow. "Which is why this bus needs to hurry up. I need to get home."

"Blizzard?" Lark glanced at the faces around her. "Who says there's going to be a blizzard?"

The man scoffed. "The weather bureau. Didn't you get the warning?"

"No." Snow spiraled inside and gathered in the gutters. Small ice pebbles bombarded the sidewalk, and it grew harder to see the parking lot on the other side of the road. "Do they think the roads will close?"

"It's a blizzard. Yeah, I'm guessing the roads will close."

"Don't worry." Another man offered her a small smile. "We should have time to get home first."

It wasn't a comfort. They hadn't even begun and already things were going wrong. Inching closer to the threshold, she heard the gears of the electronic doors strain. The glass panels rattled but didn't move. Peering outside, she tried to get her bearings. She wished she had paid more attention when they were here last. Everything looked so different from the maps Wren had shown her. There were a few scattered buildings. Shrike would already be on a rooftop to the right. The perfect vantage point to watch the road. Wren was in the gated area to the left. Floodlights washed over the buses parked in perfect rows. She could make out the guard booth by the entrance. There was a red light on top of it that flashed as a bus driver activated the automated gate. Metal squealed against metal as the gate opened and the bus entered. It soon disappeared among the other buses and snow. She jumped when her phone began to buzz. Wiggling her thumb out of her mitten, she answered the call.

"Hey," Lark said. "Did you know that a blizzard was going to hit tonight?"

"Of course not," Wren said. "Are you all right?"

"So far, so good." Moving closer to the door, and further away from the crowd, she lowered her voice to add. "Well, apart from the storm that might snuff out any fire we try to start."

"We've got fuel. It'll burn, I promise."

"If you say so."

"Hold on, I'm getting Shrike to join the call."

Biting her lips, she listened to the clicks and beeps, suddenly desperate to hear her sister's voice. A quick glance around reassured her that no one was paying attention to her. Anyone who wasn't talking with a friend was watching the road, willing their bus to arrive.

"Lark?" Shrike's voice crackled through the speaker. "Are you all right?"

Lark smiled. "I'm okay."

"I'm all right, too," Wren said.

"I've been texting you this whole time. Settle down." The call buzzed, and Shrike cursed.

Lark winced in sympathy. "Are you really cold?"

"I'm on a rooftop with an inch of snow on my back." Shrike added a heartbeat later, "I can handle it."

Leaning across the threshold, Lark eyed the distant building. The one closest to the highway. "Is there at least a windbreak?"

"A little one." Another gust of wind crackled through the speaker. "I haven't seen anything out of the ordinary. Wren, anything new?"

"All quiet where I am," he said. "A few drivers have come through. No sign of the security guard."

"You remember what I told you to tell him if he finds you, right?" Lark asked. "And remember to make eye contact. You always look so shifty when you lie."

Wren grumbled. "I've got this."

Lark bounced in place, trying to generate some warmth. "Hurry up, Trent. I'm losing feeling in my legs."

"Poor you," Shrike said.

"Well, at least the cold will help distract me from my crushing guilt," Lark said.

"What do you have to feel guilty about?" Shrike asked.

"We broke Barsotti," Lark said. "You get that, right? We might have actually driven him insane."

Shrike snorted.

"We left him thinking that we didn't see anything," Lark said. "That would really mess with his head."

"He'll get over it," Shrike said.

"Or we've given him a mental breakdown," Lark said.

"Wren, back me up," Shrike huffed.

"I have to side with Lark," Wren said.

"What?"

"He just looked so defeated," Wren said.

"That's not our fault," Shrike said.

Lark shrugged. "It kind of is."

"It definitely is," Wren corrected. "He was under a lot of pressure, and we didn't help. Honestly, I don't know if he'll recover or if he's just going to spiral. Either way, we need to leave town before he gets interested in us again."

"I've already changed over our license plates," Shrike said. "We'll change them again once we leave the city. It should make it a bit harder for him to track us."

"I still can't believe you stole someone's plates," Lark said.

Her sister snorted. "Really? Petty larceny is where you draw the line?"

"Dad wouldn't approve," Wren said.

"He also wouldn't have liked us selling the wedding rings to bail the truck out, but he would understand," Shrike declared. "At least we'll have it to get through this storm."

"We'll eventually have to get rid of the truck altogether. Wren might not have faith in Barsotti, but I do. He's stubborn. And he's a lot smarter than he lets on. He's going to come after us," Lark said.

"And that's why I don't feel guilty for messing with his head," Shrike said.

"Not even a little bit?"

Shrike's voice was as hard as stone. "Lark, we had to sell the rings because of him."

The wedding bands had been the only things they'd had worth anything. It would have been too much of a risk to put the charge on a credit card. They had found the nearest pawn shop after Barsotti had let them go. It had been a quick sale. Lark had handed the rings over with a slight smile and a wistful shrug but hadn't been able to convince either sibling that she was okay with their loss.

"We have other things to remember them by back home," Lark said.

Shrike grunted.

"Barsotti was just doing his job. Rather excessively, but still." Lark rolled her shoulders and began to pace. She was frozen to the core. "He must have seen something really bad, right? I mean, for him to be this obsessed. What do you think happened to him?"

"It's not our problem," Shrike said.

"No, but it adds to my guilt. Maybe we should leave him a letter explaining everything."

"We'll take care of Trent. That can be our apology." Shrike's tone changed in an instant. "Here we go. There's three buses incoming."

Lark looked toward the distant road. Even with the streetlights, it took her a moment to spot the approaching vehicles.

"Which one is Trent's?" Lark asked.

The phone line went silent.

"Shrike?" Lark pressed.

"Damn it," Shrike growled. "I can't read the numbers."

"Lark—"

Lark cut her brother off. "I can do this."

"We didn't really account for such a lack of visibility," he said.

"Trust me."

"Guys, I need a decision here," Shrike said.

"We're sticking to the plan," Lark said.

Wren hesitated. "All right. Let's do this. Still breathing?"

The sisters dragged in deep breaths and repeated the mantra.

"I'm heading to you guys," Shrike said and ended the call.

Wren followed. Lark instantly felt alone. Her chest constricted until it was hard to pull in another deep breath. Shoving her phone back into her pocket, she watched the buses draw closer. One after the other, they turned into the depot. There was no going back now.

# Chapter 12

Shrike shook the snow off her pocket binoculars and made one last attempt to read the bus numbers. Even with the snow forcing them into a slow crawl, it was impossible. The small ledge that ran around the edge of the building gave her something to duck behind as the vehicles passed along the road below. Once she was sure they had passed, she rolled just enough to shove her binoculars back into her pocket. Grabbing her duffle bag, she slid herself back from the edge. The motion forced her snow gear to bunch up. The cold bit painfully into her stomach. Sucking in a sharp breath, Shrike distracted herself by mentally retracing the route she needed to take. They had carefully mapped out the path through the clustered buildings to make sure she could get into her second position in time.

Snow toppled from her back as she pushed herself up. The cold had sunk through the layers of her winter gear. It had made her muscles stiff. Her joints hurt as much as her wounds and her feet had gone numb. Squirming back behind an air-conditioning unit, she packed up her bag and kicked out her legs, trying to get some sensation back. Fumbling with the last pocket, she felt her heel strike something solid. Something made of flesh. Shrike snapped her head up. She had kicked a tiny snowdrift. Exhaustion was starting to play tricks on her brain. Then she realized that she had crawled into the shadow cast by the air-conditioning unit and she began to doubt if she really was alone. Drawing her knees up to her chest, she searched the rooftop. There was nothing but the gathering snow. Between all the preparations and her lingering fear that the demon might track them through their dreams, Shrike had refused to sleep. It was costing her now. All her thoughts were clouded, and it was growing harder to think. Sitting with her back pressed against the cold metal of the unit, she began to doubt her senses.

Blindly, she pulled her bag closer. It was stuffed full of garlic bulbs. She was never going to get the smell out of the fabric. Even the cold couldn't stop the stench. Adrenaline strummed through her veins and left her trembling. She had been waiting for her anxiety to drop but it just wouldn't. It was never like this. Once they had a plan, once she knew exactly what was expected of her, everything else fell away. Nothing mattered but getting the task done. There was clarity in it. Shrike clenched her jaw and tried to smother the squirming sensation in her chest. It didn't work. Her thumb inched across her phone's keypad. One touch and the autodial would call her father. *He's not there to answer,* a voice in the back of her mind whispered. Cursing under her breath, Shrike got to her feet and started toward the fire exit.

Jamming her phone into her pocket, she rushed across the rooftop. A small platform connected the back of the building to the external fire escape. Frost had already started to coat the spiral metal staircase. Pulling the duffle bag strap onto her shoulder, Shrike gripped the handrail and started down. The staircase rattled with her thunderous footsteps. Halfway down, her foot hit a patch of ice and she dropped onto one knee. Something twisted in her gut, and she looked up. Snow whipped past and blotted out her view. From what little she could make out, there didn't seem to be anything standing at the top of the staircase, but she still felt like something was there. Gripping the rail and keeping her eyes on the connecting platform, she stood. She strained to hear anything other than the howling wind. A fine tremor shook the railing against her palm. Something else was on the staircase.

Unable to see anything above her, Shrike glanced below. Nothing seemed to be there either. Freezing in place, she waited for the next footstep, hoping to get a sense of where the unseen thing was. And which way she needed to go to avoid it. Snow flashed across the distant floodlights, casting a thousand whirling shadows over the world. Darkness gathered on the edges of her vision. She whirled back and forth but couldn't get a proper look at what was circling her. Pulling the bag off her shoulder, she wrapped the strap around her hand and held the bag before her. It was a feeble shield.

A dark shape raced past her shoulder. She spun toward it. Her heavy snow boots caught on the edge of a step. Grabbing the railing, she managed to stop herself after falling only a few steps. White-hot pain sparked through her ankle, and her knee twisted. Draped against the railing, she felt the metal vibrate again. She still couldn't tell if it was the growing wind or if something was rushing toward her. Grinding her teeth against the pain, she sprinted down the stairs, the bag held before her. Sweat began to gather along her hairline and her lungs burned. At the last twist, she jumped the rail. Landing in a crouch didn't dull the pain of the impact. Shrike choked down a cry. She pushed her hair back from her face and looked up. The random thumping stopped. The staircase stilled. Turning on her heel, she sprinted deeper into the clustered buildings.

Shrike staggered on, one arm lifted to shield her eyes from the pelting ice and brutal wind. Ducking her head, she forced herself to blindly follow her set path. Random patches of black ice hid beneath the drifting snow. As she rounded a corner, her heel caught another patch and she fell. Her knee drove into the concrete. Pain shot up her leg and sparked in her hip. Shifting shadows whipped around her like a flock of ravens. They seemed to darken with every passing second. Light flashed between the buildings. The slowly moving buses had almost reached the main entrance. She was supposed to be in her second position by now. Fear created a cold lump in her throat as she thought of Lark and Wren facing Trent alone. Her knee clicked as she got up and ran through the maze of buildings. Her hip spasmed and twitched. The constant threat of another ice patch kept her from picking up her pace.

Making one last turn, Shrike came to the bus yard's office building. She fixed her eyes on the back door and charged forward. The shadows closed around her like a thousand living creatures. She threw herself against the thin door, her weight and momentum cracking the feeble latch. The door opened, and she staggered inside and glanced over her shoulder. There seemed to be something wrong with the shadows. There was life to them. Shrike slammed the door shut and started down the long hallway.

The hallway was brightly lit and had the lingering scent of disinfectant. It was a small reassurance that the cleaners had already been here. Crouching low, she crept past the series of office doors, her footsteps muffled by the thin carpet. It was so cold that she could see her breath. The air shifted behind her. She spun around. Nothing came rushing toward her. Turning back, she caught a glimpse of a shadow passing across the hallway. She hesitated, unsure if she had really seen it. Wren hadn't contacted her about the guard. Not knowing the man's location put her on edge. She needed to take care of him but her already limited window of opportunity had just gotten slimmer. With one last glance behind her, Shrike decided to follow that retreating shape. The lights flickered as she moved silently down the hall. Reflexively, she tightened her grip on her bag and cradled it to her chest. Nothing had spiraled beyond their control yet, but she felt it coming and it left her shaking.

Drawing closer to the doorway the shape had slipped through, Shrike slowed her pace, pressed against the wall, and listened for movement. There was only the wind and the low muttering of a TV. She peeked inside. It was an empty staff room. She eyed the full pot of coffee that had been left to grow cold on the burner. The lights were off, but the wall-mounted TV was still on. Either the guard was coming back, or they had left in a hurry. Unwilling to enter the shadows, she started to go when the emergency news broadcast caught her attention. The storm was due to hit earlier than expected. They were suggesting all residents get home as soon as possible. Shrike watched the broadcast with sinking dread, trying to decide if this gave them more time or robbed them of it.

Pulling her phone out, she hurriedly typed out a text to Wren. If the guard hadn't left already, he could be doing his last rounds and that would take him to the guard's booth. His reply came an instant later; Lark was okay. She was waiting for two of the buses to approach the depot. The third had already entered the parking lot. Trent wasn't the driver. Wren still hadn't seen the guard. The reminder of how close Trent was to her siblings sent a new wave of fear coursing through Shrike. The decision was made in an instant. The guard could be left as a loose end. If he did involve himself, she'd do what it took to keep her siblings safe. She had always known that she could kill for them. Somewhere behind her, a door slammed. Shrike spun around, her heart lurching into her throat. She braced her feet and squared her shoulders. At the far end of the hallway, the broken door thudded against its frame. The lights flickered, allowing the shadows to consume patches of the hallway. The cold deepened, and she no longer felt alone. Turning on her heel, she sprinted to rejoin her siblings.

***

Wren stared at Shrike's last message, barely suppressing the urge to call her back. Neither of them needed the distraction. Huddled in the corner of the guard's booth, tucked out of sight of the windows, he watched the security monitor flick through the different cameras. He breathed a little easier when Lark reappeared on the screen. Her hot pink coat helped him keep track of her. A stray car had cut in front of the buses along the road. It gave them a little more time. Wren watched his sister hug her bag for warmth. She was nervous. The urge to call her again hit him hard, and he quickly shoved his phone into his pocket. His hands shook with a mixture of adrenaline and caffeine. It was still getting harder to keep his eyes open. Hours without sleep was taking its toll and the space heater wasn't helping. At first, he had felt guilty being the only one that got to stay warm. Now he was too comfortable. He smacked his cheeks in a desperate attempt to fight off the fatigue.

"Just a few more hours, Wren," he told himself sternly. "You can do this. You need to do this."

It seemed that the buses were rigged with sensors that triggered the gate since none of the drivers needed to punch in a code. Between the system and the weather, the night guard hadn't had much of a reason to venture out from the main building, so all of Lark's prepared excuses for why he was here were going to waste.

"Unless he's heading out here now," Wren mumbled. He rubbed his hands over his face. "Shrike's going to find him. She'll take care of it."

All Wren had to do was stay in the camera's blind spot for the next few minutes. It was a small blessing that the cameras were focused on the gate rather than the interior of the security booth. Wren jumped his shoulders and tipped his head from side to side, trying to wake himself up. It was almost time. He had to move soon. The thought shook him out of his stupor, and he realized that he had been mindlessly staring at the security footage. It had already switched to a different camera. Trent was coming, and he had lost track of Lark.

"Damn it," he muttered and scrambled up.

He dropped back out of sight when the latest driver raced past the booth. Like the others before him, he didn't linger in the compound. The man didn't even glance toward the booth as he passed through a side gate and darted across the street. There weren't many cars left in the staff parking lot. Carefully, Wren pushed back up and peered out the window that faced the main building. It was snowing harder than he had thought. While it wasn't hard to spot the buses, the people gathered in the doorway were little more than splotches of color. He flicked his attention from one pink jacket to another as the vehicles crept closer and the small crowd grew restless.

"Come on, Lark. Where are you?" His breath fogged up the glass and the temperature dropped.

Wren had hoped that they wouldn't need to use Lark like this. All Trent had to do was bring the bus into the lot like all the other drivers did. But Ruckus Robbie's accusation had changed things. If the demon was using Trent's job to access victims, it wouldn't want to jeopardize it by hunting on the clock. Between the lack of security and the independence of the drivers, Trent had the perfect opportunity to keep his bus for a few hours after his shift without raising suspicion. He could leave just as quickly as he came. They needed him to stay. In Wren's ideal world, Trent would come on his own. Using Lark to lure him was a backup plan. And he hated himself for putting his little sister into that kind of danger.

His breath caught when the first bus pulled up in front of the main entrance and people hurried out. Some darted into the building to catch the coming train while others scattered into the parking lot. At the same time, the people that had been waiting rushed onto the vehicle. It was already pulling away by the time the last bus approached. Lark was the only one left. Pressing closer to the glass, Wren tried to keep track of her.

"Just keep driving, Trent," he begged on a whisper. "Don't see her. Just drive right in."

He could only watch as the storm worsened, and the world was gradually consumed by a white haze. The floodlights helped a little. He could still make out the general shapes of the buildings, but all the details were lost. Ice crystals gathered on the windows and shadows began to form. A thin icy mist crept into the booth. Shivering, he stood up and leaned against the cold glass. Cupping his face to block out the light, he peered into the snow, tracking the approaching headlights. His glasses fogged. Yanking them off with one hand, he rummaged in his pocket for his handkerchief. Something smacked against the side of the booth, hard enough to make the overhead light sputter. Dark shadows lurched through the mist. He squinted, trying to bring them into focus. Something hit the roof. Crouching down, he fumbled his gloved fingertips over his lenses and pulled them back on. His breath caught as he tried to find Lark again.

"Oh God," he whispered and ducked lower.

The thick snowfall made it hard to judge distance. He could barely see the fence anymore let alone the main building. Lark's pink coat was gone. A dark shape rushed past the window. Wren jumped back, his breath catching in his throat. His heels knocked the canisters of gas he had siphoned from the buses. Wren ducked to stabilize them and tried to remember the stories Lark had told him. The door didn't open. No guard came bursting in.

"Lark."

He inched back to the window and searched for her again. His blood ran cold when he noticed the dark figures squirming over the parking lot. The mangled limbs clawed at the concrete. They disappeared into the haze as soon as Wren looked at them. He flattened himself against the window and strained to see what was out there. Dense shadows emerged from around the parked buses. Like the writhing limbs, they were there but not. He rubbed his thumb over his glasses. As if getting rid of the smears would somehow solidify the shapes. The things lurched and swayed. Broken creatures lumbering aimlessly toward the gates. They dispersed like fog when he looked at them directly.

"No," he whimpered.

All his plans were focused on Trent. He didn't know what to do if there were other demons hiding in the storm. Trembling, he tried to think. There wasn't enough information. All he knew was that these things didn't move like Trent did. They were something different.

"If they're there at all," he said as the shapes flickered across his vision.

That scared him more. It was his job to think things through. To know what's going on and what they should do about it. His family was relying on him to do just that. But he didn't know anything. Movement drew his attention back to the building and his stomach dropped.

"Lark."

He pushed down his fear and looked for the final bus. It was still there by the curb. Either Trent would soon be coming over, or he had left the vehicle behind to chase Lark on foot. If it was the first, the gate had to stay open. If it was the second, he needed to lock it down now and cut off his exit. Wren glanced to the control panel. If Trent came and found the gate locked, he'd leave and they would have lost their best chance to kill him. He didn't know what the right choice was. He needed more information. The security cameras weren't any help. The snow made the footage look like static. Grabbing handfuls of his hair, he forced himself to take a deep breath and decide.

"Lark will get him here."

Wren lunged for the control panel and flicked the switch. The gate locked with a dull thud. He grabbed the two containers of gas and shuffled for the door. The contents sloshed wildly, the weight and motion throwing him off-balance.

"Get it together, Wren," he ordered himself.

Shoving one container under his arm, he fumbled with the latch. The door flew open, and the wind surged inside. The sudden cold hit him like a sledgehammer. He struggled to breathe as he ran into the shadow-ridden night.

# Chapter 13

Lark fiddled with her phone as she paced across the threshold. Normally, these types of adventures made her feel powerful. Like she was in control of the whole world and everyone in it. Tonight, she just felt like a worm squirming on the end of a hook. As the people had rushed around her, it struck her again that this was the first time she was bait for someone dangerous. At least, she could embrace her fear. There was no need for her to hide it. The demon would know. It was probably better it did. Like chumming the waters. Standing in the threshold, she could barely see the buses that were pulled alongside the curb. She lingered and counted the vehicles again.

"Three," she said softly, her brow furrowing.

There shouldn't be three. She swore two had already pulled away. Peering into the white haze, she counted again. The vehicles evaporated before her eyes only to reform. Each recount came up with a different number. The wind picked up, driving the snow deeper into the building. The glass doors rattled, and the gears cranked, the dull noises reminding her that she was alone. She hadn't been the only one to shrink from the buses. None of the strangers had shown any sign that they knew what had arrived. Most of them had looked confused by their own actions, but they had listened to their instincts and backed away from the door. In that moment, everyone knew that *something* was very wrong. They had gotten over it quickly, though. Everyone had run forward the moment the bus doors opened.

"And then two of the buses left," she said to herself. "No. That's not right. One of them kept going."

Peering into the snow, she recounted the buses. *Only two.* Her thoughts stopped when the chill hit her again. It was so cold it hurt.

Bouncing on her toes, she rolled her shoulders and forced herself to step outside. She had already wasted too much time. Shrike and Wren were waiting on her. She needed this to be over. The swift wind gathered the snow into uneven mounds. She stumbled over them even as they buried her feet. A random gust stripped the warmth from her bones. Hugging her backpack, she hunched her shoulders and ducked her head.

Now there were three buses. They seemed solid. Real. There was a bit of distance between each vehicle. About a car length. Just enough space that she wouldn't be able to stand beside one and still see the other drivers. Picking the wrong bus would give Trent time to slip away. Or creep up behind her. Her eyes darted among her three options. She supposed that it was smartest to check the middle one first. At least that way she would have a straight shot back into the building. She glanced behind to reassure herself that the doors were still jammed open—they were. She vaguely wondered if Shrike was responsible.

A shadow streaked across her peripheral vision. She spun around but there was only the white haze. Snow crunched under her boots. Lark pulled up her jacket hood and peered into the white air, inching ever closer to the glowing lights of the middle bus. It emerged like a mirage. Another shadow caught her attention. Not a formless blur like the other one. Someone was walking through the blizzard beside her. She turned, expecting to see one of the strangers from before. The shape disappeared. She picked up her pace and clutched her bag so tightly that her fingers shook. There was movement inside the bus. Basic details gradually came into view. The driver's seat was occupied, but she couldn't tell if it was Trent. Lark kept her eyes on the dark shape as she inched closer.

Hitting a patch of ice made her stumble. She only looked away for a second, but it was enough. The driver was gone. The bus idled before her, its lights on and the driver's seat empty. Lark's stomach dropped. She turned and spotted someone standing just on the edges of visibility. They were too tall and gaunt to be Trent. She turned to face them, and the shape disappeared into the snow. Spinning around, she tried to find it again and noticed a different shadow. There was something wrong with this one's proportions. Its limbs were elongated and so was its head. She couldn't gauge their height. She couldn't even tell how far away it was. It didn't seem to notice her. The creature stalked away and disappeared. Still, she knew it was nearby. She knew she wasn't alone.

Her phone suddenly felt heavy in her pocket. All she had to do was hit one button. Speed dial would do the rest and Shrike would come running. She wanted to pull out her phone. She wanted to run. Slowly, she turned back to the bus. The driver's seat was still empty. The rest of the seats weren't. The passengers were just dark silhouettes pressed against the fogged glass. Fear and indecision twisted up her insides. She couldn't be sure of what she was seeing, but there was a chance that she was looking at Trent's intended victims. Lark had seen what a demon could do to a human being. She couldn't just let it happen.

Keeping a tight grip on her bag, she darted forward, stumbling over the snow. She was a second away from jumping through the open doors when something deep in her chest twisted up tight. Swallowing thickly, she threw herself back and quickly looked around. The primal instinct wouldn't tell her where the predator was. She only knew that it was close. Panic buzzed in her chest as she spun in a tight circle.

Lark forced herself to breathe slow and deep. Dread remained a heavy weight against her chest. The cold air burned her lungs, her eyes watered, and her ears throbbed. None of it mattered when she felt something watching her. She slowly forced herself to look up. The bus windows were empty. Lifting her gaze a little more, she saw the deformed figures standing on the roof of the bus. More of the creatures emerged from the haze. None of them disappeared. They were creatures of shadow but somehow seemed as solid as flesh.

Backing up a few more steps, she spotted another figure in her peripheral vision. It didn't look human. It was something else. Something gnarled and twisted. Its spine was so hunched that it was almost broken in two. There were others behind it, but they were harder to make out. They were a barely visible horde lumbering mindlessly across the sidewalk. Something rushed at her from the side. She screamed and threw herself back. Ice and snow tripped her up and she fell.

Gripped by panic, she squeezed her bag instead of breaking her fall. Pain blurred her vision. Fighting back another cry, she scrambled up and turned back to the bus. The sidewalk was empty. All three vehicles were gone, but the shadows remained. They shambled around her. It seemed like they didn't see her. She wasn't going to wait for them to find her. Getting onto her feet, Lark turned to run back to the building.

"Hello again."

She screamed. Turning toward the voice, she found Trent standing only a few feet away, unbothered by the gathering storm. His arms hung loose by his sides and his veins bulged against his skin. When the wind changed, she choked on the stench of his rotting flesh.

"Were you looking for me?" Trent smiled.

Lark trembled violently. She clutched her bag until her arms went numb and slowly straightened. It was time for her to do her part and bring this night to an end, one way or another.

"Where are your siblings?" Trent asked. Drool seeped from the corners of his mouth as his smile widened. "They didn't leave you all alone again, did they?"

The dark shapes inched closer while never gaining any detail or definition.

"You don't have anything to say?" Trent asked. "That's all right. I don't need you to speak."

She clearly had Trent's undivided attention. Now she had to put it to good use. Spinning on her heel, Lark sprinted for the main building. She didn't dare to look back. She didn't need to. She knew the man and shadow creatures were following. Threading her arms through the straps, she pulled her bag onto her back. A sharp tug secured the pack flush against her spine. The chafer fuel cylinders bounced painfully against her back as she burst through the frozen doors.

Lark gripped the safety rail and rushed down the stairs, her wool mittens catching on the frost that now coated the metal. The snowflakes swirled around her boots. She didn't see the patch of ice until it was too late. She was too cold to move properly, so when her feet slipped out from under her, she couldn't keep her hold on the handrail. The world spiraled as she toppled down the stairs. Pain exploded within her. She felt the edge of every step crack against her bones and the metal chafers made it worse. Blood splashed over her tongue. With one final thud and an agonized yelp, she reached the bottom of the stairwell.

Icy tiles burned against her cheek. Everything hurt. Something hot welled against her mouth. It took a second for her fog-riddled brain to realize the warmth came from her bleeding lip. *You have to get up!* Lark swore her father was screaming in her head. *Lark, go! Now! He's coming!* She hadn't realized that her eyes were closed. Forcing them open hurt and the pain sharpened her mind. *Darling, get up and run.*

"Daddy?"

Amused laughter washed over her. She blinked rapidly and pushed up onto all fours. Trying to brush her hair from her face made her tip to the side and she frantically braced herself again. Solid thumps echoed off the walls, and her skull throbbed in time. Lark twisted just enough to see up the staircase. The sloping roof blocked her view but, as she watched, Trent slowly descended the stairs. There was a sharp clack and whirl. She could assume that the automatic doors had finally closed. *Go,* her father's voice urged. She obeyed. Pushing herself up, Lark darted into the tunnel. Her lungs burned. Blood dripped down her chin and she struggled to lift her feet.

"Where are you going?" Trent called after her. "The next train isn't due for a while. We're all alone down here."

The words propelled her on. Rushing down the tunnel, she felt the stock images watching her again. Their dead eyes bulged out toward her. The lights buzzed and sputtered, allowing shadows to dance over the walls. Lark locked her eyes on the bathroom door and ran as fast as she could. Trent's echoing footsteps always sounded right behind her. Without hesitation, Lark threw herself against the door. Shrike's precautions worked and the door opened easily. Stumbling inside, she raced to the back of the long room, passing by a row of stalls that seemed to swell with shadows.

Behind her, the door creaked open. She didn't look back until she had entered the last stall. Trent stood in the doorway, still smiling, a visible chill coiling around his legs. She threw the stall door closed and flipped the feeble lock.

"Are you serious? You think that's going to keep me out?"

Lark kept her attention on the window. She had to climb onto the back of the toilet seat to reach it. There was a small pit beyond. It was just big enough for her to climb into. From there, she could stand, push aside the metal grating, and scramble her way back to street level. That was if Shrike had remembered to break the locks. Otherwise, she'd be trapped. Wrenching open the window, she swept aside the gathering snow and pulled herself up. As she closed the window behind her, she glanced back to Trent. She prayed he was gone. She hoped he was still following. The stall lock flipped, and the door swung open. Trent saw her in the pit and laughed. The sound gutted her. For a split second, terror froze her in place. Then he took a step toward her, and she lunged up.

The metal grating flopped easily to the side. Lark gripped the edge of the pit and tried to pull herself up. Her muscles strained until they trembled, but she didn't have the upper body strength to lift her weight. At her feet, the window creaked open an inch, allowing a dark shadow to slither out. It brushed against her legs like living mist. Lark screamed. Tears burned her eyes. In blind panic, she kicked out. Her feet scraped against the wall and her arms trembled. Using every ounce of her strength, she dragged herself out of the pit. Scrambling on all fours, plowing through the gathering piles of snow, Lark threw herself into the glow of a floodlight. *Still breathing?* Her father's voice hovered in the back of her head.

"Still breathing," she whimpered.

Forcing herself back to her feet, Lark ran into the maze of parked buses, barely able to see them through the driving snow. She didn't look back. She knew the demon would follow.

# Chapter 14

The wind chilled Lark's sweat-covered skin. Every step was a strain as her feet sunk into the soft snowdrifts. Every panted breath froze her lungs. The storm whipped the snow past the floodlights, making shadows strobe over the vehicles. As she lumbered into the rows of parked buses, shadow beings seemed to slip through her peripheral vision. She couldn't tell if they noticed her or not. Occasionally, the buses blocked just enough of the wind for her to hear her boots crunching through the snow.

Ice snapped behind her. She whipped around. Snow gathered in the creases of her coat as she strained her senses. A dark mass darted from behind the bus, crossed over the gap, and disappeared behind the next vehicle. It moved so fast she hadn't had time to scream. Still, she knew what she saw. It was the living shadow that had tried to grab her in the window pit. The formless mass with long clawed hands. She staggered closer to one of the buses and crouched down, trying to get out of sight, and waited for Trent to appear. To follow the grotesque blob. He didn't.

*It's not a part of him,* she realized with growing terror. *It's something else. A different breed. Did Wren plan for there to be more than one kind of demon here? What if fire doesn't kill this one?* She squeezed her eyes shut and forced down a deep breath. *Don't panic. He'll do his job if I do mine. I just have to get Trent to the right bus.*

Her eyes snapped open as the thought hit her. If this thing, whatever it might be, wasn't attached to Trent anymore, it was hunting her independently. It was possible it had spotted her and was now circling around to trap her. Lark lowered herself to the ground and peeked under the buses. All the flickering shadows seemed lifeless.

Normal. *Where is it?* Her breath caught. *And where's Trent? Did I lose him?*

Ice matted the fur edges of her hood as she looked back toward the subway. His shadow swept across the ground. His heavy footsteps crunched through the snow gathering near the rear bumper. A few more feet and he'll enter her row. He was too close. Lark ran deeper into the yard, sprinted down the almost clear aisle, and darted into another row. She had to force herself to stomp randomly into snow piles and create a visible trail. She wanted distance, but she needed him to follow.

She made it two more rows before spotting the Blob again. It glided around the buses with unnerving ease, its needlelike fingers clawing at the ground. It slipped behind a bus. Lark bent over, trying to catch sight of it under the bus. The wind eased and, for one second, it was possible to hear the chafer fuel containers clattering around in her backpack. The Blob stopped. There was a loud crash, and a bus skidded a few inches. It rocked on its suspension, the hiss and groan lost as the wind picked up.

*Was that the Blob or Trent? Or is there something else? How strong are they?* The questions swirling through her mind came to a grinding halt when the Blob slithered back the way it had come, tracking her down. Lark retreated down the row, heading back toward where she had last seen Trent. Rounding the rear of the bus, she glanced behind. Trent's shadow poured out into the aisle. She threw herself behind the nearest bus just as the wind died again. Pressing herself against a huge wheel, she clamped a hand over her mouth to muffle her heavy breathing. Trent's footsteps stopped. The slithering fell silent. Lark and the monsters all froze in place, each straining to hear the others.

Barely daring to move, Lark glanced down. With the buses acting as windbreakers, the snow was gathering along their sides and within the rows. The aisles were swept almost clear. There weren't any obvious footsteps to give her away. But if they looked in the row, it would be easy to tell which direction she went. Still, they didn't move. None of them did until the next gust of wind. Lark headed deeper into the yard, unsure how far away either demon was.

Random pauses between the gusts allowed her to hear Trent's footsteps. They were louder than they should have been and seemed heavier with every strike. Like he was somehow growing larger. Glancing over her shoulder and checking around corners, she never saw him, but he sounded so close. She darted out into an aisle before spotting the Blob out of the corner of her eye. Staggering back, she turned. Trent's shadow stretched out over the aisle behind the buses. She was trapped within the row, with the demons closing in on either side.

Tugging her bag off her shoulders, Lark crawled around the front wheels of the nearest bus, where the wind had swept it bare. At least bare enough to hide her tracks. Stomach pressed against the cold ground, she scrambled into the shadows. It wasn't that dark. She could still make out shapes and dull colors. Still, the dim light terrified her almost as much as the things she was hiding from. She swore something was squirming against her as she burrowed into the powdered snow gathered beneath the vehicle. Lark shoved more snow on top of her, trying to bury herself, and peeked out into the row. Her footprints reminded her how easy it would be for them to find her hiding place. Just when she decided it would be better to slip out the other side and keep running, Trent entered the row.

His footsteps drew closer. It was impossible to keep completely still as the snow encased her. She clenched her jaw to keep her teeth from chattering. Holding her breath, she peeked over the low snowdrift. The glow of the floodlights still seemed to flicker, the quick bursts of light flashing against metal and ice. Windswept snow slowly erased her footprints. Unable to hold her breath any longer, she released a small gasp. Her heart sank when the Blob slithered into view. Its shadow melted into Trent's as he stalked closer. She spotted his boots and prayed that he'd keep walking. The two creatures met right in front of her hiding place.

Lark's lungs burned and her body ached as she tried to keep quiet. Blood rushed through her ears. It was so loud; she couldn't understand how they didn't hear it. Her fingers twitched within her mittens. The tiny motion reminded her she didn't have her backpack. Panic seized her. She craned her head back as much as she dared, searching for where she had left it, and her stomach dropped. A strap had caught on a bolt. The bag half-dangled from the undercarriage, hiked up just enough that it rattled with the heaving wind.

Tears burned her eyes as she glanced back to Trent. He hadn't moved. Neither had the Blob. If they took more than a passing glance, they'd surely see her. All they needed was a reason to look. They were so close now. If the wind died, they'd hear the metal chafer containers click together as they resettled. They'd know, they'd look, and they'd grab her before she could get out. Her stomach clenched so tight she felt acid burn the back of her throat. Slowly, carefully, Lark stretched out one hand. The tips of her mittens brushed over the side of the bag. All she had to do was wedge it into place. Keep it quiet until they had gone. She stretched a little further and tapped the bag again. It swayed, slipped free of its hook, and dropped onto her hand. Instinctively, she grabbed it and dragged it back behind the wheel. She glanced away for a split second to make sure it was tucked in the shadows. When she looked back, Trent's boots had turned toward her.

Cowering under the snow drift, Lark froze and watched Trent slowly lower himself onto one knee. *My coat's pink*, she remembered. *My coat is bright pink*. She was buried within snow and shadows and still felt unmissable.

Trent lowered a hand. He didn't seem to feel the cold as his fingers sunk into the snow. With the extra balance, he hunched a little lower, pressing into the shadows under the bus. He was too close. Her body ached to run. To scramble out from under the belly of the bus and sprint for her siblings. The knowledge she wouldn't get far didn't dampen the impulse. He'd be on her before she could even shake off the snow. A tear trailed down her cheek as a childish voice whispered in her head: *I want my dad.*

Trent slammed his free hand against the side of the bus and pressed in a little more. He was close enough now that she could see the blood seeping from the corners of his eyes. The droplets froze on his lashes before they could fall. Veins bulged under his skin, and he reeked of death. Frozen in terror, it took Lark a second to realize how much trouble he was having moving his rotting eyes. They jerked and twitched, but he had to move his head to scan the area. She flinched when he shoved his hand into the snowdrift. His fingertip came to a stop an inch before her face. Close enough that he would feel the warmth of her breath. He slipped his torso under the bus. Only the few inches of snow covering her back separated them. Lark was too afraid to move. Too afraid to scream. She could only watch his eyes twitch and wait for him to look down. He didn't. A second later, she realized that he *couldn't*. His decaying eyes didn't have that range of motion.

Before the idea could settle in her head, Trent pulled back. The bus rocked with the force. The show of strength chilled her. *He's just messing with me. He saw me and now he's going to lift it up and crush me under the wheel!* Lark closed her eyes and prayed that it would be quick. But the rocking eased to a stop. Trent's thunderous footsteps slowly moved to the front of the bus. Then he kept walking. Lark's eyes snapped open in disbelief. *It's a trap. It has to be. A sick little game. He's waiting for me to come out.* Craning her neck, she scanned as much of the aisle as she could see. He was gone. *But he was right there!* The howling wind surged up and covered the sounds of his footsteps. *How did he not see me?* An image of his eyes emerged in her mind. *How much can he actually see?*

There was so much she still didn't understand. The only thing she could hold onto a certainty was that Trent's body was decaying. It wasn't the craziest idea that this would affect how well the demon could use it. *Or it's a trap,* a voice whispered in the back of her head.

She looked back to the row and choked on a scream. While she had been distracted by Trent, the Blob had inched closer. Its dark form blotted out the light. Long, spiderly arms grew and shrunk back into its body as it crawled above her. Its nails scraped against the undercarriage. Keeping still, Lark watched it drag itself from one side of the bus to the other. An arctic chill radiated from its undulating body. Lark lifted her hand from her bag, making sure her trembling fingers didn't move the chafers, ensuring that she didn't make a sound. The creature paused. Even though it didn't have a head, she knew it was listening. *That's how it's tracking me. That's why they didn't care about my footprints. It's all about sound.*

Her lungs burned for air and her head swam. Still, she refused to breathe. Suddenly, the Blob shot forward, scrambled across the undercarriage, and slithered off. Lark pressed her face against her shoulder and tried to smother her sobs. She couldn't do this anymore. It was too much. She was used to luring people away from unseen dangers. Every instinct she had begged her to stay where she was. Or run. She wasn't built or trained to deal with this.

*You need to go now.* The whispered voice sounded like her father, and it made her heart ache. *I don't want to die.* She knew he couldn't really comfort her. He was gone and all she had left was a memory of his voice. *Wren and Shrike are waiting for you.* Swallowing the lump forming in her throat, she tried to drown out her father's voice. *The Blob heard something. It heard them. They don't know it's coming. You need to go. Sweetie, you've got to do this. Your siblings are counting on you.*

Lark drew in a deep breath, grabbed her bag, and obeyed her father. She had almost dug herself free when she heard a solid but dull thud. Before she could even lift her head, the power cut out. The floodlights died and the world plummeted into darkness.

\*\*\*

Wren staggered to the side, fighting to keep his balance. Carrying cannisters of sloshing gas made it harder to navigate the growing piles of soft snow. He was trying to readjust his grip when the floodlights flicked off. Everything seemed different in the dark. The air felt colder. The wind pushed harder. And the buses on either side of him transformed into looming dark pillars. Snowflakes gathered on his glasses to blur his already limited vision. He blinked rapidly, hoping that his eyes would adjust to the dark. He wasn't far from the bus they had earmarked for the trap, and he was already struggling with the cannisters. Squinting into the darkness, he lumbered on.

The bus he had chosen was at the center of the yard. In theory, it would keep all of this a safe distance away from any bystanders. At the very least, they'd have more directions to flee in. He had anticipated that the demon would cut the power. He only hoped it was to try and scare Lark and not because it was suspicious. Wren tightened his grip on the cannisters. His fingers were quickly growing numb. He wasn't sure how much longer he could hold onto them. Pain dug into his shoulders. The petrol was a lot heavier than he had anticipated. Shuffling around one more bend, he spotted the bus they needed. Frost had gathered along its metal side and the folding front door rattled with every passing gust. Wren had broken the lock before syphoning the tanks. Trudging a bit closer, he noticed the low but wide snowbank that was rapidly building alongside the vehicle. Lark might not have a problem with the door but getting through that drift could be an issue. It would definitely slow her down. Wren decided to dig it out a bit once he had everything else ready.

Removing the lid on the first cannister unleashed the harsh stench of gas. After fumbling with the heavy containers for a moment, he changed tactics and dug a few holes into the snowbank. It let him pour the gas under the bus just by tipping it. Once they were lighter, he could do the other side. He was working on his third hole when he noticed movement behind him. He spun around so fast he fell back against the bus, the cannister sloshing over his lap. He shoved the cannister off but wasn't quick enough to keep the gas from seeping under his jacket. It was a few seconds of chaos but, when he looked back up, nothing was there. Wren wiped a gloved finger over his glasses and pulled his hood tighter around his face. His vision was still smeared, but he could see a little deeper into the shadows. Nothing moved but the wind.

He went back to work. Going over the plan again for the thousandth time helped to steady his nerves. After he set the trap, he'd hide beneath the neighboring bus and wait for Lark to come. She would use the broken door to get onboard. She'd make sure to lure Trent on with her. She'd get him to the middle. It would be tight, but there should be enough time for Wren to get out and seal the front door with garlic while Shrike got Lark out through the emergency exit at the rear. Then Wren would light a flare and set the petrol on fire. He absently patted his jacket pocket. A mournful smile pulled at his lips as he squeezed the roadside flare.

Their father had celebrated each of them getting their driver's license with dinner at a waffle house and a fully stocked emergency kit. It hadn't just been for big events. The man had loved safety checks and waffles and had indulged in both to invent a long-standing tradition. The flare Wren had in his pocket had come from Shrike's kit. Joe had replaced it a few days before he died. He wanted them to be ready for the long drive back home. In a way, their dad would be the reason this demon burned. It seemed fitting.

The cannister was now empty. Digging deeper into the snowdrift, Wren shoved the empty container under the bus and turned to the next one. A shadow moved behind him and the bus swayed on its suspension. He whipped around. As he squinted into the darkness, the wind picked up and a few more buses began to rock. A cold mist rolled in. The deathly, unnatural chill that they had always felt in Trent's presence. It gathered between the buses and dropped the temperature until his body heat was enough to fog his glasses. He tried wiping them clean a few times but soon gave up. Licking his chapped lips, he decided he had wasted too much time. It took both hands for him to lift the second cannister. He half dragged it to the back of the bus, where the wind had swept the snow clear, and kicked it over. The dark liquid glugged out over the black ice. He watched it for only a second before running to get into his hiding place.

The hair on the back of his neck prickled as he crouched down beside the neighboring bus. Ice snapped. On one knee, he looked around him, his panted breath fogging his glasses. He couldn't see much in the dark mist. Maybe something moved. Maybe it was just a trick of the minimal light. His chest tightened so hard he gasped. He took it as his primal instincts warning him of a coming predator. It was different from the fear that Trent provoked. Duller somehow. More like what he had felt when he had seen the creatures lumbering past the security booth. *Maybe they're demons too,* he thought. *Maybe that's what they look like when they're still hunting for a host.*

Fear twisted up his gut until bile splashed over his tongue. Bracing himself against the side of the bus, he dry-heaved. Smelling his gas-soaked sleeve had him gagging again. Suddenly, seeing the world as a cluster of dark smears made him seasick. Cursing under his breath, he pulled off his glasses and hurriedly wiped them off on his jacket. While he had barely been able to see with them, being without was worse. Shapes moved all around him. Closed in on him. Huge shadows that towered over him like giants. Another crack of ice had him fumbling to get his glasses back on. The shapes vanished as if they had never been there. It took him a second to hear anything but the wind and his panicked breaths.

Footsteps. Heavy, booming footsteps. They were coming closer. Standing back up, he leaned out into the aisle, trying to get a glimpse of what was coming. It struck him a second later that this wasn't what he was supposed to do. It wasn't what his siblings needed him to do. Dropping onto his knees, he burrowed through the snow that had gathered beside the large wheel. There wasn't much room to maneuver, and he hit his head a few times as he twisted around. Lying flat on his stomach, the flare clutched between both hands, Wren locked his gaze on the broken door and muttered a curse. He hadn't cleared a path through the snowdrift. It had already grown an inch taller. *Lark's so little. She's delicate. How is she going to make it through that?* Images of Trent catching her while she struggled to enter the bus filled his mind. He started to push himself forward but stopped when the bus above him rocked. The footsteps were closer. Trent was almost here. They had to stick to the plan.

The cold mist crept into his hiding place, taking away what little warmth he would have gotten for getting out of the wind. The broken door rattled violently. He squeezed the flare tight, took a sobering breath, and waited.

\*\*\*

Frigid air rushed through the open door and turned Shrike's skin to ice. Shielding her face with one arm, she blinked into the darkness. The highway streetlights were glowing dots in the haze. To the side, the subway was still lit, just like the building she was standing in. Everything else was dark. The floodlights that had illuminated the parking lots, drop-off area, and bus yard were all dead. Even the red light that sat atop the security booth by the gate was off. Without them, she could barely see the nearest row of parked vehicles. It was the perfect place for Trent to hide. Shrike retreated into the building. First, she tore off a piece of duct tape with her teeth and fastened it over the lock, ensuring they had a way back into the building if they needed it. Then she wound the duffle bag strap around her forearm. When she clutched the remaining material in her hand, the bag sat tight against her arm, almost like a shield. When she let go, the strap uncoiled and the duffle bag dropped to the ground. She wished she had more time to test it. To make sure that she wouldn't get caught up in the strap if the worst happened. But she was already late. Pulling her hood tightly around her head, she charged into the storm.

It didn't take long for her to reach the first row of buses. They emerged from the mist, towering over her in a way that they shouldn't, suddenly appearing three times their size. They were covered in ice crystals, their wheels half buried in the snow. Unwilling to slow down, Shrike cautiously glanced all around her as she jogged down the row. The vehicles swayed in the wind. She flinched every time she heard the suspension groan. A part of her was convinced that they were going to topple over and crush her. It was getting harder to tell the difference between the ice reflecting the dull light and demonic glowing eyes.

Tightening her coat against the wind, she picked up her pace. Random patches of black ice caught her heels and made her slip. Shrike fumbled but managed to keep upright. The deeper she went, the more she started to wonder if this damage would be the thing that drew the guards out. She supposed that a power outage during the beginnings of a blizzard wasn't something that would cause alarm, but she didn't know the protocols and the uncertainty left her uneasy. *What if Trent did more than just cut the lights? Could he have taken out the subway? Warped the tracks maybe? Would the trains even still run without electricity?* The questions swirled in her head until she could barely think. She found it surprisingly easy to clear her mind of the clutter. She just ran faster and told herself that Wren would figure it out. He was the smart one. He probably anticipated this happening from the start.

Rapid heavy footsteps caught her attention. They were loud enough that she could just hear them over the howling wind. Sliding to a stop, Shrike listened as she caught her breath. Each time she heard them, she spun toward the footsteps. The sound was always gone by the time she had turned. The wind pushed aside just enough of the fog that she realized she had slid into the middle of an aisle. All around her, buses swayed and groaned. Turning slowly, she spotted something moving through the darkness. Years of hunting made her body move without thought. She darted to the nearest bus, careful to stay downwind, and sunk into the piled snow to keep out of sight. She tightened her grip on her duffle bag and moved it behind her body. There might only be a feeble amount of light, but she wasn't going to risk it catching on the metal fastenings and giving her away. Her focus narrowed on the spot where she had been standing. As the footsteps drew closer, she realized that there were two sets. Only one of them was running. Her blood ran cold when Lark sprinted down the aisle.

The wind had pushed back her hood and ripped apart her braid. Lark's long dark hair whipped around her. It would be so easy for the demon to grab a handful and bring her down. It was clear she couldn't keep her speed up for much longer. Lark turned to look over her shoulder. Unshed tears glistened within her wide eyes and Shrike's heart clenched. That wasn't a show. It wasn't fake. Shrike knew when her baby sister was terrified. She wasn't luring Trent. She was running for her life. And all Shrike could do was hide. It gutted her to watch Lark turn in tight circles. She staggered one direction before changing her mind and going another. She turned in tight circles as the booming footsteps drew closer. Her heated breath created a fine mist around her as she turned with indecision. A thunderous crash made Lark pause. She stumbled a few steps before getting the rhythm right. Then she was running and soon disappeared back into the darkness. *She's going the right direction,* Shrike told herself. *She's okay.* The thought died the moment she spotted Trent.

He strode through the minimal light, his footsteps booming like thunder. The silver mist followed him and there was something curling around his legs. It was dark and formless. But there was something about it that made Shrike certain it was alive. Trent rounded the edge of the bus and the shadow creature coiled out. Shrike watched in horror as it rapidly slithered in the direction Lark had fled. *It's hunting her,* Shrike realized.

Trent paused. Snow gathered in his hair; the flakes as white as his flesh. His veins stood out like wires against his skin. His unblinking eyes were discolored, and his lips had begun to shrivel back from his teeth with rot. He looked like a marionette made from a slowly decaying corpse. Shrike stood frozen in horror as Trent stalked down the aisle.

*Oh, God, what are we doing?* Shrike asked herself. The thought lingered with her as she slipped behind the bus and ran to get into position.

***

Lark hit a patch of ice and her feet slipped out from under her. She landed on her back, the chafer containers digging painfully into her spine. Biting her lips, she managed to muffle her pained scream. It was still too much noise. The Blob must have heard her. Rolling onto her hands and knees, she looked back down the dark aisle. Trent's footsteps echoed toward her, but he and the Blob remained in the shadows. Scrambling onto her feet, she glanced around, trying to orientate herself. She should have reached the trap by now unless she had taken another wrong turn. Her heart skipped a beat when she spotted a bus with a small object plastered on its side. It was just above the piling snow but still too low to be at eye level. She tried to rush toward it and pain shot down her spine. She had bruised something in her fall. Limping to the bus, she found a souvenir magnet stuck to its side and almost sobbed in relief. It was the right bus. She pulled off the magnet, stuffed it in her pocket, and hurried around the front bumper.

A gust of wind brought the stench of gasoline. It was gone in a moment, and she found herself sniffing the air, hoping to catch it again. That stench was a promise that Wren was nearby. She wanted to look for him. She wanted her brother. She couldn't stand to be alone another second. But her siblings were counting on her to do what she said she would, so it didn't matter what she wanted anymore.

Slamming into the snowdrift in front of the door knocked her off-balance. She dropped to her knees rather than fall flat on her face. The loose snow reached her waist. Blindly, she reached out and hit the door's central joint. The door rattled and jammed. Breath catching, Lark looked up and pushed again. This time, the door folded a little bit, barely an inch, before jamming again. Dragging herself onto her feet, she peered through the haze. A thin layer of ice encased the hinges. She batted at them, cracking them apart, and tried again. It wouldn't open.

Trent's footsteps echoed over the wind.

Trying not to panic, she shoved her hair back from her face and took a proper look at the door. Only then did she notice that the top of the snowdrift had covered the bottom runner. Lark swiped at it with trembling fingers. Wearing knitted mittens had been a bad idea. Snow had gathered between the stitches, and they weren't insulated enough. Her fingers were so cold she thought they'd snap if she tried to bend them. The wind worked down to her sweat-dampened thermals and she could feel that same brutal chill creeping over her skin. The approaching footsteps made her work faster. Once the track was cleared, Lark pounded both fists against the door. It rattled and jerked to a stop. Panicked, she threw her shoulder into the joint. It still wouldn't open. Trent's footsteps echoed around her. Drawing back, she rammed herself against the door. Ice crunched and the door jerked open a few more inches. It was almost enough. Grabbing the edge, she pulled and shoved until her arms shook and sweat beaded along her hairline. The door groaned but opened a little more. Just enough for her to slip through.

Lark tossed her bag in first then squeezed through the gap. The arctic fog followed her inside. There were only three metal steps to climb but Lark had to hold on the handrail to drag herself up. With all the windows closed, the bus had managed to hold onto a little of the heater's warmth. The few degrees of difference were both comforting and agonizing. It hurt to have her blood rushing through her veins. Lark's legs gave out, and she dropped onto her knees. Her fingers felt broken as she pulled her bag closer. Once she had it resting against her thigh, she tried to open it. Her hands wouldn't work. She couldn't grip the zipper through the frozen wool of her mittens. Trent's booming footsteps were closer now. Sobbing, she bit the top of her glove and yanked her hand free.

The brutal cold attacked her bare skin. Her joints felt like shattered glass as she finally grabbed the tab and opened her bag. She dumped the chafer containers out and hurriedly unscrewed the lids. Trent was walking faster now, his footsteps ringing like a death toll as she forced the containers open. The bright pink ethanol gel had survived the weather without freezing over. All it took was a few forceful shakes to have it drip from the containers in a slick glob. She smeared it with her gloved hand. First over the steps and handrails then over the door hinges, careful not to touch the glass. She couldn't risk Trent seeing it.

Shuffling on her knees, she worked her way deeper into the bus, smearing the gel over everything she could reach. She threw herself against some of the seats to try and line the windowsill. The gel didn't have a scent. The darkness masked the color. She shoved the empty containers back into her backpack. Working fast, she sloppily marked the interior. She realized too late that she had also lined the back exit. The door she was supposed to leave through. She didn't have time to worry about it. Trent had stopped walking. She had been conscious of the sound but hadn't tracked it enough to know if he had passed by.

Keeping low, she crept back to the front of the bus and peeked out the windshield. Snow was already refilling her footprints. Pushing up a little further, she pressed closer to the glass and peered into the darkness. The shadows swirled. The tip of her nose pushed against the icy glass. Her gaze scanned over her footsteps again, and she realized that they weren't all hers. The trail came too close to the bus and the dashboard blocked her view. Bracing herself against the dashboard, she rose onto her toes, trying to see where Trent had gone. The hair on the back of her neck prickled. Someone was watching her. Darkness loomed in the corner of her eyes. She turned. Trent stood in front of the doors, separated from her by a few feet and a thin layer of glass.

Trent smiled. His teeth weren't human anymore. They were gnarled and stained with blood. She screamed and threw herself back. Her legs smacked against the driver's seat, and she toppled down. Trent slipped his hand through the gap and slowly coiled his fingers around the edge of the door. He made sure that she heard each long, sharpened nail tap against the glass. Lark scrambled over the back of the driver's seat. Her bare hand couldn't grip it properly, and she dropped heavily onto the front passenger seat. She slipped over the gel and hit the floor, losing sight of Trent as she became wedged between the seat and the driver's booth. Pressing herself to the floor, she tried to catch sight of him, but the mist was too thick. Ice snapped, metal groaned, and glass cracked. The whole bus rattled as Trent forced the door open.

Lark squirmed into the aisle and scrambled onto her feet. The bus rocked violently to the side and tossed her onto the seats. The suspension groaned. Metal buckled. Hurling herself up, Lark glanced back to the door. Trent climbed the stairs. Behind him, the door slammed shut with enough force to shatter some of the windows. The blizzard surged through the hairline cracks. Frost grew over the walls, the floors, the seats. Lark gripped the handrail to steady herself. It was so cold that the metal stuck to her. She peeled off a layer of skin, yanking herself free. The chill followed her as she retreated to the back of the bus. Trent's echoing laughter made the floor tremble beneath her boots. As the frost gathering on the windows smothered the minimal light, she realized that her siblings weren't going to be fast enough. The temperature plummeted, and she was alone, in the dark, with a demon.

# CHAPTER 15

Shrike raced toward the rocking bus. Its suspension groaned and its tires skidded across the icy ground. Lark's screams pierced the wailing wind. Shrike couldn't understand. She thought she had been barely a step behind Lark. But she had somehow gotten turned around and now she could be too late. Pushing herself faster, Shrike sprinted for the rear of the bus. The metal sides bulged out in places and the windows shattered as she neared. Shrike used the bag to shield herself from the flying shards. She didn't see the patch of black ice until she had stepped on it. Momentum made her slide forward. Peeking around her bag, she spotted the back of the bus careening toward her, the rear bumper set to crush her skull. Shrike stomped her feet against the ground and kicked off. It wasn't graceful, but she managed to skid just out of reach of the rear bumper and into a snow pile. Before she could catch her breath, the bus buckled on its suspension and slid back across the ice. Shrike rolled out of the way of a coming tire. Lark screamed again. Shrike got to her feet. She caught a glimpse of Wren as the vehicle skidded over the ice. Ripping open her bag, she fished out a lanyard of garlic bulbs and blindly tossed it toward him. He would get it on his own. Lark needed her more.

The back window was still intact and covered with a thick layer of frost. A hand thudded against the glass, its nails clawing streaks through the ice. Suddenly, the bus seemed full of shadowy limbs that coiled around each other and scraped across the frost. It was impossible to tell if any of the writhing limbs were her sister. The bus slid again, and something hit the interior walls. Shrike released the bag strap from around her arm and hooked it over her shoulders. It pressed against the wound on her neck as she studied the swaying bus, trying to get the timing right. It swung back toward her, and she surged forward. Bits of glass crunched under her boots, giving her just enough traction to move on the ice and jump onto the rear bumper. Pressing herself against the cold metal, she gripped the corner with one hand while grappling with the emergency release. Her gloved fingertips worked around the latch. She yanked hard. The door didn't open.

Lark screamed, and Shrike pulled again. The latch flipped up like it should but the door still wouldn't open. Shuffling closer, she clutched the handle with both hands and threw her weight back. It still held solid. The bus trembled and bucked. Shrike pulled herself back against the siding to keep from getting thrown off. Cheek pressed against the metal, she glanced up. *There'd be an emergency hatch on the roof.* The walls were smooth, and the back window was still intact. The moment the bus stilled again, she jumped. All she needed was a few extra inches so she could grab the edge of the roof. Despite her gloves, she managed to get a decent grip. Her shoulders flexed and pulled against her stitches as she dragged herself up. The vehicle rocked. Each jolt tore her skin open just a little bit more. Blood soaked into the back of the thermal under her shirt. Hooking a leg over the edge, Shrike climbed onto the roof.

Staggering to keep her balance and half blind with the snow, she worked her way up the bus. Finally, she found the raised hatch. Squeezing it between her thighs, she endured the rocking and swaying of the bus, searching for the release latch with trembling fingers. She found it and yanked hard. Frost shattered. Pulling until she shook with the strain, she forced the hatch up. Shadowy hands pushed through the gap and clawed at her legs. She ground her teeth, readying herself for the pain. It didn't come. The taloned fingers tried to burrow into her thighs, but they dispersed like smoke the moment they touched her.

She tugged on the strap, sliding the barrel of her duffle bag toward her legs. The hands retreated as the garlic-filled sack drew closer. She hadn't completely zipped it back up after throwing Wren a lanyard and a few bulbs slipped out. They toppled through the hatch and the hands evaporated, allowing her to finally see inside the bus. Even with the storm rushing through the busted windows, there was an oppressive gloom. Something colder and thicker than the blizzard itself. A hazy fog coated the floor. In a second, she saw where it was coming from. Trent wasn't human anymore. He twitched as his bones snapped and grew, twisting into a deformed monster. His skin peeled away in tendrils of freezing mist. His muscles had withered against his bones. The haze poured out from his elongated arms to create bat-like wings and his curved spine scraped against the ceiling. The bus was too small for what he had become. He had to rip up the interior to move at all. Lark used that small advantage as best she could, scurrying and crawling and keeping just beyond his reach. She was running out of room. The demon lashed out, ripping a few chairs out of the flooring. Lark screamed and ducked out of sight.

As the bus lurched, Shrike spotted Wren. He stood by the door, frozen in terror as he gaped at Trent's new form. He must have already hung the garlic because all he held was the single unlit flare.

"Do it!" Shrike ordered.

Wren flinched and looked up to meet her gaze. At the same time, Trent squirmed, dinting the metal walls as he tried to find her. She kept one unopened packet of garlic with her and dumped the loose bulbs into the hatch. The demon unleashed a high-pitched scream that drove into her ears like ice picks. The sound snapped Wren from his daze. He lit the flare. The narrow, steady flame was blinding within the darkness.

"Wren!" Shrike screamed as the bus trembled. "Now!"

"But Lark—"

"I'll get her!"

That was all the reassurance Wren needed. He stabbed the burning head of the flare through a gap in the door and set the chafer gel alight. Then he tossed the flare under the belly of the bus. It only took a moment for the golden flames to grow. They melted the snowdrifts and lashed at the metal walls. Shrike leaned through the hatch. She hadn't thought the fire would take to the gel so quickly. Blue flames had already crossed from the door to consume the driver's seat. They spread along the smeared gel like grasping fingers. The ice that coated the walls began to melt but it didn't douse the flames. Trent unleashed another feral earsplitting shriek and threw himself toward Lark. He had to cross under the hatch to reach her. Getting too close to the garlic was like hitting a brick wall. His huge body was thrown off-balance. He staggered back before falling against the burning wall. The bus rocked and the flames spread. Lark fell into the aisle with a startled yelp.

"Lark!" Shrike screamed. "Up here! Hurry!"

She pounded the roof until her little sister finally looked up. Shrike flattened herself against the top of the bus and leaned through the hatch, stretching as far as she could. Lark scrambled onto a seat as the fire spread onto the vinyl. The smeared gel made her slip, and her boot caught the flames. The demon got up. This time, he purposefully hurled himself against the unseen protection of the garlic. The whole bus lurched with the impact. The back wheels popped, and the bus dropped onto a sharp angle. Lark clutched the burning seat to keep from getting thrown back into the aisle. Small flames sparked on her mitten. She quickly battered it out with her bare hand.

"Lark, come on! We don't have much time!"

Lark stood on the back of a seat and reached for her. They were too far apart. Shrike stretched until her shoulder ached. Lark scrambled over the seat, barely avoiding the flames. The demon had already destroyed the next chair in the row, so she didn't have a backing to climb up on. She could only push up onto her toes and stretch her body out. Shrike shifted her hips a little closer to the hatch and reached down again. She had to grip the edge with one hand to keep from falling inside. Their fingertips brushed and the demon swiped out again. It wasn't a frontal attack. Instead, he pounded the flooring until he broke through and had to retreat from the flames. In the same moment, the sisters realized what he had done. The constant battering had rolled the garlic bulbs a few feet back. The demon now had the room it needed to swipe a giant wing across the bus. Lark dropped against the burning seat. The boney, winged limb crashed into the wall, making the bus slide on its rims. Embers burst into the air. They sparked and swirled within the creature's mist. It retreated with an unearthly wail.

"Get out of there!" Wren screamed. "The fire's spreading too fast!"

His panic spurred Lark into motion. She pulled herself up, locked her eyes on Shrike, and scrambled over the seats. The demon raged. It threw its hunched back against the roof and crushed the seats under its wings. Lark jumped forward onto a pile of smoldering wreckage, bringing herself closer to the demon. She jumped as the broken items slipped out from under her. The sleeve of her jacket was alight when Shrike grabbed her arm, her gloved fingers snuffing out a few of the flames. Unable to let go of the latch without falling in, Shrike tightened her grip and began to drag her sister up. Sweat dripped down her neck, the salt burning as it welled within her stitches. A few airborne embers settled against their jackets, finding trace amounts of gas and chafer gel to feed on. Small flames littered them both, and the roof was starting to grow warm by the time she managed to get Lark up. Lark grabbed the edge of the hatch the moment it was within reach and tried to help. She did little more than stabilize herself while Shrike pulled her the rest of the way out.

Lark hurriedly crawled away from the hatch. The wind whipped the small sparks on her jacket into a crackling flame. Shrike manhandled her little sister out of her snow coat and tossed it back into the hole. It landed on the demon's head, momentarily blinding it. Shrike hooked the bag of garlic over the hatch rim and slammed the lid shut.

"Shrike!" It was hard to tell if it was the heat or the brutal cold that hurt her more.

Shrike pulled off her jacket. The icy wind knocked the air out of her lungs. "Put this on."

"But you'll freeze," Lark said.

Another gust of frigid air stripped the warmth from Shrike's bones. Her muscles turned to stone and shook so hard she couldn't breathe. Still, she managed to put Lark into the oversized coat. There wasn't time for her to argue. The bus was already growing unbearably hot, the demon was screaming, and Wren was begging them to move.

"We're out of time!" Wren bellowed. "We need to get out of here before the gas tank lights up! Get down here now!"

Whatever Trent had transformed into, he could still understand them. Wren's warning sent him into a frenzy. He slammed against the sides of the bus with renewed strength. Shrike threw herself onto Lark, pinning her against the metal as the bus skidded violently to the side. The rear crashed against the neighboring vehicle. Shrike scrambled to find something to hold onto. They slid a few inches but weren't thrown off.

"Go," Shrike told her sister.

Lark wiggled out from under her, and Shrike turned back to the hatch. The bag of garlic was still trapped there, but the impact had popped the hatch door open. She slammed it shut again and searched for a way to lock it. Smoke spewed around the edges, tainted with the scents of roasting garlic and burning flesh. She gagged as metal heated beneath her. The air was growing hot enough that she could almost bear the bitter cold. Still holding down the hatch, she twisted around to see where Lark had gone. Lark had circled around to the front of the bus and now stood at the edge, just above the door. She was peering down at Wren as he tried to convince her to jump into a snowbank.

"I could break my ankle," she said.

"Burning to death is not the better option, Lark!"

Shrike was about to suggest she jump onto the hood first when the demon slammed its wing through the windshield. The entire vehicle trembled with the impact. Thrown to the side, Shrike lost her grip on the hatch. The lid flipped up, and she had to brace herself against the edges to keep from falling inside. She instantly had the demon's attention. It contorted its grotesque form until it was facing her. Mist coiled out of its empty eye sockets even as the flames clung to it. With a high-pitched squeal, it charged toward her. Its elbow joint crunched against the roof and its exposed spinal cord slashed through the metal.

Ice splinted from its body as it cracked open its jaw and bared its fangs.

Shrike scrambled back as the sudden rush forced new waves of heat and smoke through the gap. The bus bucked and thrashed. The bag of garlic started to slip. She threw herself onto the hatch and tried to force the lid back down. They needed to keep the demon sealed inside. The spinal cord glided through the roof like a shark fin breaching the surface. With only a few feet left separating them, it dipped back down out of sight. Shrike crawled onto the hatch lid.

"Where did it go?" Her throat burned and her eyes watered as black smoke billowed through the cracks. "Wren! Can you see it?!"

She rose onto her knees and searched for her siblings. Neither of them had moved. Lark was still just above the door. Wren was still trying to get her to jump. Shrike decided to just tackle Lark and force her over but, before she could move, the bus lurched to the side, slipped over the melting ice, and careened toward Wren. Lark's scream was drowned out by the sickening crunch of metal on metal. The edge of the bus bucked up and it slammed against the neighboring vehicle. Lark was knocked off her feet and fell back against the hot metal.

"Wren!" Shrike screamed. "Wren? Where are you?"

Shrike leaped from the hatch. Lark met her at the edge and both women dropped to their knees. The buses were wedged together so tightly that the smoke barely passed through.

"Wren!" She glanced to Lark. "Did it get out of the way? Can you see it?"

"I don't know."

The two women braced themselves as the demon lashed out again. With a burst of flames, the bus was forced back. They crashed against the bus on the other side and ground to a halt. The impact almost sent them both over. Peering through the smoke and wind, Shrike noticed something half buried in a snowdrift. Wren had gone back into his hiding place beneath the neighboring bus.

"Wren!" Lark screamed.

He lifted his head. Snow coated his glasses, and his body shook.

"Move! Now!" Shrike ordered.

His feet slipped over hidden black ice as the demon threw itself around the bus, making its second attempt to crush him. Wren scrambled over the ice and snow. The bus raced back toward him. Grabbing the mangled wheel with one hand, Wren dragged himself forward. He collapsed into the aisle just before the flaming bus slammed back against his hiding place.

"I'm okay, I'm okay."

Wren's hands trembled so badly he could barely wipe the snow off his glasses. The demon screamed in fury, the shrill cry shattering the few nearby windows that were still intact.

"Run! We'll be right behind you!" Shrike ordered as the bus bucked.

Snapping out of his shock, he glared up at them. "I'm not leaving you. Just jump already! It's going to bust its way out and that tank is going to blow!"

The demon heard this. Unwilling to let the girls go, it threw its now-massive body back and forth, forcing the bus into constant motion. Embers and snow swirled on the billowing smoke. The metal rims squealed, and the suspension groaned. The sisters barely had time to regain their footing before they were tossed against another bus. The flames surged up with every impact, urged on by the lashing wind. Shrike and Lark could only hold onto each other as they slid around on the heated metal.

Flames shot up, and Shrike braced her feet. The heavy rubber soles forced them to a stop and, when Lark mirrored her older sister, they were able to awkwardly lurch and tumble through the thin wall of fire. They toppled over twisted metal, the torn edges slashing into them, and flopped onto the roof of the neighboring vehicle. Shrike pressed her cheek against the cool metal, heaved a sigh, and forced herself to move again.

Clambering up onto all fours, she first checked where the demon was. Despite the smoke, the bus burned so brightly that it hurt to look at it. She could just make out the dark silhouette of the demon thrashing within the golden flames. The damage had spread further than she had thought. Carried by the wind, the embers had scattered over the bus yard, finding hundreds of small gas spills to ignite. A handful of buses were already burning and the refueling station on the far side of the lot was surrounded by spitting embers.

"Oh, God," she mumbled. "We have really messed up."

"What?" Lark asked.

Airborne sparks rushed toward a pair of gas pumps. The sisters ran but didn't make it to the front of the bus before the vehicles crashed together again. Lark slipped forward, toppled down the windshield, and fell on the hood. Shrike staggered to the side and fell over the edge. She would have landed in the flames had the demon not sent the bus skidding again. She slipped between the two vehicles and dropped onto the asphalt.

The piled snow barely softened the fall. Her bones rattled, and the air rushed from her lungs. Shards from the broken windows littered the ground. They slashed at her cheek and dug into her as she squirmed. The sliding bus had compacted the snowdrift, creating a small dam that kept the gas from spilling further out. Shrike had destroyed half of it. What remained protected her from the heat. But as she tried to get up, she felt how flimsy the remaining half was. One wrong move and it would all come crashing down. Without the blizzard, she would already be burning. Bracing her hands, she carefully tried to push herself up. Pain shot along her back. Her arms buckled, and she slumped against the snow. Smoke flooded her lungs. She coughed as her muscles spasmed.

"Shrike?" Lark called.

Her voice sounded so soft against the constant grind of metal and roaring flames.

"Shrike, come on!"

Glancing over her shoulder, she saw Lark trying to get to her. Wren was holding her back, keeping her away from the burning bus that still thrashed and rocked.

"Shrike, please, you have to get up," Lark sobbed. "Wren, get off me! We have to go get her!"

The front of the bus whipped around like an angry snake. The twisted metal blocked Shrike's view of her siblings. Clenching her jaw and pressing her forehead against the ground, Shrike pushed up. Every muscle twitched with pain. The burning bus skidded toward her, bringing with it an unbearable heat. She dug into the piled snow beside her to get under the neighboring vehicle. Flattening herself against the ground, she covered her head and braced for the impact. The bus rocked and swayed. Simmering wreckage scattered around her. She looked up in time to see a metal shard crash down onto the snow. It created a small groove for the gas to trickle through. Sparks flew around her. A few settled on top of the liquid but fizzled out before it could ignite.

Adrenaline surged through her veins, and she scrambled for the opposite side of the bus, clawing her way through the piled-up snow. The demon squealed. She could hear its body piercing the metal walls to strike the bus she was hiding under. The ground trembled. The bus bounced and rattled. She crawled faster but couldn't escape the growing heat and lingering stench of gas.

"Shrike?" Wren bellowed. "Where are you?!"

She was panting too hard to answer. Sweat dripped from her face. Blood soaked the back of her shirt. Her leg grew hot as small fires broke out over the material of her pants. Lifting her leg to try and keep it from any puddle of gas, she burrowed into the snow, dragging herself forward by her hands alone. Her back collided with the undercarriage of the bus. The bus rocked again and a stray bolt raked across her shoulders, gouging into her bite mark. She couldn't keep in her scream. Blinking through the tears, barely able to move the injured side of her body, she pressed on.

A gust of wind struck her face. She flinched back before realizing that a hole had opened in the wall of snow before her.

"Wren? Lark?"

Wren's face filled the hole. His relieved smile fell when he noticed the embers skittering around the gas tank and the liquid slowly trickling under the bus.

"Lark! I found her! Help!"

Shrike crawled forward to her siblings as they tore apart the snow wall. Wren reached inside and grabbed her arm. She was too heavy. He couldn't pull her out in an easy slide. It was more a series of sharp jerks that almost dislocated her shoulder. The moment she was free, Lark dumped handfuls of snow onto Shrike's burning pant leg, quickly smothering the flames. The pressure made her scream.

"I'm sorry, I'm sorry," Lark said. "Almost done."

"Get her up," Wren said.

He tightened his grip on her arm and dragged it over his shoulders. Even after Lark took the other, it was a struggle to get Shrike upright. With the adrenaline and fear, she hadn't realized how bad her leg was until she tried to put pressure on it. The charred edges of her pants scraped against her fresh burns. Her knee gave out and she slumped against her siblings. Lark and Wren grunted and pressed closer to her sides. They struggled with their height differences as they pulled her down the aisle. Without the fire, Shrike was battered by the full force of the storm. The wind cut through the layers of her thermal getup and pressed in through the holes in her pants. It didn't even ease her burns. The pellets of snow smacked against her tender flesh like needles.

Wren looked around, trying to orientate himself. The sound of the explosion hit them a split second before the pressure did. They staggered and fell, their ears ringing and a burst of heat singeing their backs. Shrike tried to hunch over her siblings as flaming debris rained down around them. It was over in a moment. They turned and a second blast knocked them over. They twisted around to look. The blasts had ripped the vehicle apart. Barely any of it was still intact.

"Oh, God," Lark whispered.

Wren readjusted his glasses, the firelight catching on the lenses. "I may have underestimated a few things."

"Do you think it's dead?" Shrike asked.

She huddled closer to her siblings even as the air grew a little warmer.

"Of course," Lark immediately insisted. "It has to be dead. I mean, nothing could survive that, right?"

"Unless it got out," Shrike said.

Lark stiffened. "But it couldn't have. We sealed it with garlic."

"Well, we don't know if garlic still works when it's roasted," Wren said thoughtfully.

"It was cutting his way out," Shrike reminded them.

The siblings glanced at each other. In unison, they looked up at the swirling clouds.

"If it got out, it'd run. I mean, we almost killed it. Why would it come back?" Lark forced a smile. "Right?"

Shrike noted the colors of the clouds and mist. "This storm is the perfect camouflage for him. We'd never see him coming."

"It doesn't matter," Wren snapped. "Right now, we have to get you inside before hypothermia sets in."

"It's not so cold anymore," Shrike replied.

The words jerked Shrike and Lark from their shock. They looked around and, for the first time, really noticed how far the fire had spread. A dozen vehicles were ablaze and the random gas spills had grown into bonfires. Without a word, Lark and Wren jumped to their feet and dragged Shrike up with them. Huddled together, they lumbered into the burning maze, each of them constantly checking the sky.

# Chapter 16

Wren stomped through the growing sludge. There were enough things burning now that the snow and ice had started to melt. Random explosions made the ground tremble. A burning wheel streaked by them like a meteor. Wren jerked back, wincing at the blinding light. He smacked against his sisters and almost brought them all down.

"Sorry," he mumbled.

"Wait," Lark called over the wind and crackling fires. "Where are we going?"

"To the front gate," Wren said.

Her brow furrowed. "It's an electric gate. Would it even open with the power cut?"

"The employee entrance should."

"But then what?" Lark pressed. "Yeah, we were going to go that way when there wasn't a storm. When we thought there'd be enough people around to make Trent hesitate. But everyone's gone!"

"We need the main road." Wren cursed as the ground trembled again. "It's a flat windswept surface. It'll be easier for Shrike to manage with her leg."

Shrike stiffened. "I can take anything you need me to."

Looking at the state she was in broke his heart. Despite the growing heat around them, Shrike's lips were blue. Her skin was a patchwork of deathly white and raw blisters. Wren moved closer, trying to shield her from the wind, as he reassessed their options. The road was the easiest path for her leg. But she couldn't take the cold much longer without risking frostbite. Still, he hesitated to backtrack through the yard. They might not make it through again.

"We need to get Shrike inside," Lark said.

"Okay, Plan B. We cut through the security office. It was warm in there when you came through, right?"

Shrike nodded. "The power was still on, too."

One of the buses burst with enough force to flip the vehicle over. Shrike pushed her siblings behind her, shielding them from the explosion. A lump of smoldering metal shot past them and obliterated the security booth. Wren looked around. The wind had forced the flames toward the opposite side of the lot. The row of vehicles nearest the mesh gate was untouched. They just had to make it through that gap and back to the buildings before the wind changed.

"Keep close to the gate," Wren said. "Come on! We need to hurry."

They organized themselves as they walked, readjusting their grip on Shrike until they could move with a bit of speed. Wren did his best to avoid touching her wounds. It was nearly impossible. It seemed like her whole back was shredded. He felt her shivering as he pulled her closer. Shrike's stride evened out as they reached the side gate. It made his gut twist up until he felt sick. Being too numb to feel her burns couldn't be a good thing. And she was only going to get colder as they avoided the fires. He pressed closer to her but doubted the outer shell of his jacket would offer much warmth.

The heavy beating of wings made him flinch. The others heard it too. Squeezing each other tightly, they kept moving and raised their faces to the turbulent sky. Snowflakes gathered on his glasses and the mist hit his face like needles. With the mesh gate almost brushing against his left shoulder, he leaned forward and glanced past his sisters. They were still separated from the burning yard by a few rows of untouched buses. Smoke and mist churned between the vehicles. Firelight clawed into the shadows like golden talons. Still, there were plenty of hiding places for something like Trent. Lark screamed and pointed over their heads, gesturing wildly to a ball of fire barreling toward them. They darted forward, trying to avoid the flaming wreckage. The fire followed them.

Their feet tangled together as they broke into a sprint. Trying to catch each other brought them all down. The fire sailed over them and crashed into the ground hard enough to crack the asphalt. Wren looked up, his face blistering with the heat. With a few powerful beats of its wings, the demon launched itself back into the sky, embers spewing from its body.

Lark looked up and pushed her hair out of her face. "Where did it go?"

Wren couldn't get his tongue to work.

"It was a bit of a bus, right? Where is it?"

Lark looked to Shrike for reassurance.

"I didn't see it," Shrike said through chattering teeth.

"It's on fire," Wren said with sinking dread. "I don't know if it even bothers it."

Shrike pushed herself up and jumped into a crouch. The sudden burst of movement drained her. Wren surged forward, catching her before she slumped to the snow.

"Oh, God, Shrike, you're not looking so good," Lark said, her small voice barely heard over the wind.

"I'm fine."

Wren knew she was in a bad way when she let him take on her weight. Lark hurried over to help him. Together, they forced their sister forward. Shrike's boots scraped through the snow until she managed to lift her feet. Once they regained their stride, she locked her eyes on the building at the end of the row and charged forward with single-minded determination. He was never going to complain about her pigheadedness again. The sound of beating wings circled above them. Sparks swirled amongst the tumbling flecks of snow.

Shrike gazed up. "Where—"

Lark shushed her and pushed herself closer. Dropping her voice until Wren could barely hear her, Lark whispered, "I didn't get a chance to say it before. I don't think demons can see very well. Both Trent and the Blob—"

"Blob?" Wren asked.

Shrike squinted at the clouds. "It's circling us."

"It probably can't see us. We have to be quiet," Lark said.

Snow, embers, and mist swirled around them as they approached the building. The firelight struggled to reach the door and none of its warmth got this far. Entering the shadows felt like diving into a pool of ice. Wren and Lark both gasped. Shrike couldn't muffle her scream. The beating wings thundered above them. Adrenaline and pain kept them running as the burning demon sailed over their heads. Heat pushed against their backs. A burst of blistering warmth that made the night feel even colder. Wren refused to look back. He kept his eyes on the door and forced his sisters to keep going. The demon arced around them and landed on the roof, raining down sparks and blocking the entrance.

Lark pushed her older siblings to switch directions. The colossal bat-like creature swung its head back and forth, trying to locate them. The storm and chaos covered their pounding footsteps. Fire ate into its frosted skin as it crawled over the roof, following them as they cut across the open area. Wren was so focused on helping Shrike that it didn't occur to him to question where Lark was going. Behind them, the demon reached the edge of the roof. With an infuriated roar, it took flight again. Wren kept an eye on the burning monster, allowing Lark to direct them. The snow thickened and coated Wren's glasses.

"I've lost sight of it," Wren said.

Shrike stumbled, barely able to keep her eyes open.

"We're almost there," Lark promised. "Just a little further, Shrike. You can make it."

Another bend and it clicked. Lark was taking them back to the bathroom window.

"Please, Shrike, just keep going. You'll be warm soon, I promise." Lark said as Shrike almost fell again. Then, while keeping one arm around Shrike, she tugged at the zipper of her coat. "You're taking this back."

Shrike growled and shook her head.

"It's my turn to handle the cold." Lark sounded eerily like Shrike as she said the words.

Another sharp tug and the jacket came loose. Without breaking stride, Lark and Wren forced Shrike back into her jacket. The cold slammed into Lark's smaller form. It clearly hurt her, but she refused to make a sound. Sparks rained over them and the siblings looked up but there was nothing but darkness. The subway's lights were still on. It illuminated the window pit even as the snow piled inside it. They headed toward the opening. Without a word, Shrike shoved Lark forward. She was too cold to protest. Dropping onto her knees, she scrambled into the pit and ducked out of sight.

Wren hit a hidden patch of black ice. Clutching Shrike, he managed to keep upright but still hit the brick wall. Dropping painfully onto his knees, he pulled Shrike closer.

"You're next."

Shrike didn't have it in her to argue. She all but toppled into the pit. After the darkness, the bathroom lights hurt his eyes. Both of his sisters seemed to disappear into the brilliant glow, leaving him alone in the dark. The shadows writhed against him like maggots. Shuffling closer to the pit, he dangled his legs over the edges. Something slithered past him before he could jump. He flinched and twisted around. Ice pellets gathered against his coat as he searched the shadows. The fire blazed in the distance and the wind howled. Curiosity gnawed at him, keeping him peering into the darkness even when he knew he should jump. He needed to know Trent was dead. That this wasn't all for nothing.

"Wren!" Shrike screamed.

An ebony mass rapidly slithered toward him, its long nails clicking against the ground. Wren screamed and threw himself into the pit. It was a short drop. Loose snow billowed around him as he squirmed, trying to get his legs through the window. Snow washed over the edge, and he looked up to see the formless creature looming over the rim. Instead of dropping down upon him, the creature lingered. Light bloomed behind it. An instant later, a frosted bat-like limb stabbed blindly into the pit. Wren threw himself to the side. The clawed tip of the wing slashed into concrete as it searched for him.

The motion kicked up the snow. The loose flakes covered his glasses and left him blind. Screaming again, he scrambled around the tiny pit, trying to keep out of the demon's grasp. Hands grabbed his ankles. Before he could fight, he was yanked forward. He slipped through the window and dropped. There was no way to brace himself or soften the impact. His shoulder cracked against the edge of the toilet. There was a sickening pop. Blinded by pain, he crumpled onto the bathroom floor, his arm hanging limply against his side.

"Sorry," Lark whimpered.

His sisters tightened their grip on his ankles and dragged him out of the stall. The sudden jerk knocked the snow from his glasses, and he glimpsed the still-burning demon cramming itself into the pit. It ripped apart the bricks and threw itself against the tiny window. Wren bounced against the tiles and screamed, clutching his injured arm. The motion stopped. They released his legs, letting them drop to the floor.

"Don't move," Shrike said, her words slightly slurred.

Her large hands gripped his shoulder. The pain almost had his eyes rolling back in his head.

"It's dislocated," Shrike said. "I can pop it back in."

All he could think about was the pain, and he tried to shove her back with his good arm.

"The demon's almost in!" Lark screamed.

Both of his sisters grabbed the front of his jacket and pulled him up. None of them could keep upright on their own. They staggered toward the door, propelled on by terror and the sheer will to live. Lark opened the door, and they stumbled out into the hallway. Wren didn't have time to relish the warmth. He checked his watch.

"We have to hurry." He barely had the energy to move his mouth.

They rushed down the hall, heading deeper into the subway. The demon squealed. The walls trembled as the demon clawed and bashed its way inside. They ran past the guard's booth as the bathroom door shattered. Rubble and smoke exploded into the tunnel. The unnatural frost followed. It coated the walls and slicked the ground as the demon barreled toward them. Wren glanced behind. It was bigger now. The elbows of its winged forearms shattered the ceiling tiles. The posters that lined the tunnel caught alight as the flaming monster lumbered by. It was closing in behind, drawing closer and closer, its heat burning Wren's skin. He glimpsed the window of the guard's booth opening and heard a man's scream before refocusing on the platform. On the tunnel. On the incoming train that should be arriving soon. He prayed that the storm hadn't delayed it. He begged that just this one thing would go right.

Lights pierced the darkness of the tunnel. Wren stared at it as he ran, not quite believing that it was there. Shrike crowded closer as the demon screamed. The ground trembled and the temperature dropped. Their panted breaths fogged before them as they kept moving. They were too slow. The demon was almost on them. There was no time for discussion. But the siblings only had to glance at each other to know what they needed to do next. They sprinted toward the tracks. The train was supposed to pass through the station to be stored for the night, so it hadn't slowed down. It was going fast enough to kill. The siblings ran for it. If they had to die tonight, they were going to go out together and they were taking the demon with them.

Wren glanced behind. The demon squealed as it barreled towards them. Lark noticed the exact moment its attention shifted from its prey. She began to scream. A broken, terrified wail that instantly had the demon fixated. Lark screamed and it didn't care about the lights, or potential witnesses, or danger it was surging towards. All it wanted, all it saw, was the three humans that had set it alight.

The demon charged forward. The train rattled closer. Fire swirled around them as the siblings gripped each other tight and jumped. Wren squeezed his eyes shut. There was a moment of weightlessness before the impact. Agony exploded within him, white-hot and all consuming.

Shrike tightened her grip on his arm and rolled them into the recess beneath the platform. The train surged past them with a deafening roar. Wind thrashed and the concrete he was pressed against trembled. There was a high-pitched squeal. Slowly, the pain and chaos ebbed away. He didn't dare move, wanting his last moments to be as peaceful as possible. Wren's eyes snapped open when Lark bellowed a string of profanities.

"We're not dead," he groaned.

"I think I broke my wrist," Lark sobbed. Sucking in a deep breath, she howled again. A long, feral wail.

Clutching his injured arm, Wren forced himself to sit up. Breathing hard, he glanced around, trying to make sense of what happened. They had made it. The huge demon hadn't been able to maneuver as fast. Blood, bone, and rancid skin coated the front of the slowing train and splattered across the tracks. Some of it was still burning, making the suddenly humid air reek of burning flesh.

"We're not dead," Wren repeated numbly.

Shrike weakly pushed at him. They had to crawl down the recessed space for some distance before they reached the end of the train. Shrike staggered to her feet. Even though she looked a second away from collapsing, she still tried to pull the others up.

"What now?" Shrike licked her lips and furrowed her brow. "I can't remember what comes next."

Wren motioned with his chin to the tunnel. "Maintenance exit. It connects onto the manhole system."

They could only move at a shuffling pace. Still, they were in the tunnel before the guard recovered from his shock enough to even remember they existed.

# Epilogue

Shrike finished her last bit of waffle, tossed her plastic fork into the travel container, and reached for her beer. The small twist of her torso pulled at the cuts and burns that littered her back. Every inch of her felt bruised. Stubbornly, she grabbed her beer bottle and gulped down a few mouthfuls. They had managed to escape the city limits before the blizzard had forced road closures but hadn't been able to get into the mountains. For the last two days, they had been trapped at a roadside motel, living off vending machines and painkillers. The roads had been plowed this morning, and they had been quick to take advantage of it. By noon, they were deep in the mountains. They bought lunch at a truck stop but didn't feel safe to stay there long enough to eat. The mountain view lookout had fewer people and no cameras.

On the opposite side of the picnic table, Lark frowned at her beer. "Isn't it illegal to drink alcohol in a park?"

"We've done worse," Shrike said before drinking again.

"You're not supposed to mix it with painkillers."

"We're using generic brand aspirin, Lark. Not the good stuff."

Lark hummed. "We really need to take Wren to a proper doctor. I know you said you popped his shoulder back in, but it seems like he should have regained more movement by now."

"We'll find someone right after we cross state lines," Shrike said.

They both turned to see if Wren had anything to add. His weak arm was in a sling, leaving him only one arm to both eat and scroll through his mobile phone.

"Wren?" Lark asked.

He flinched and glanced up. "Huh?"

"Are you all right?" Shrike asked.

"Yeah. Sorry, just scrolling through my news feed."

Lark swallowed a mouthful of waffles. "Anything new?"

"It's already old news. Apparently, everyone's fine with the theory that it was a John Doe suicide," he mumbled.

"We'll be okay. It's not like it can be traced back to us," Shrike said.

Shrike's phone began to buzz. The siblings froze and eyed it with suspicion.

"Who's calling you?" Wren asked.

She glanced at the screen and her stomach clenched. "It's Barsotti."

"Do you want me to answer?" Lark offered.

"I want him as far away from you as possible." She rejected the call. He instantly called again.

"We should see what he wants," Wren said.

She huffed and answered the call. "What do you want?"

Barsotti's voice was light but measured. "Where are you?"

"Why?"

"Because I have a few questions to ask you."

"And you can't do that over the phone?"

The line went quiet for a long moment. "What was the thing chasing you through the subway?"

Shrike glanced to her siblings. "What?"

"Don't," Barsotti warned.

"I don't know what you're talking about."

"You cut the yard's security cameras. The ones in the subway were still recording."

Shrike didn't know what to say so she kept quiet.

"Damn it, Shrike. Talk to me. What was that? Why was it after you? And why the hell did you choose to jump in front of a train rather than come to me for help?"

"I don't know what you're talking about."

"I have the tape. I know it was you three. You kind of stand out." Drawing in a deep breath, he lowered his voice, as if he didn't want to be overheard. "That thing... It has human DNA."

Her blood ran cold. "Oh, really?"

"You know who it was," he said. "Do you know how he got like that?"

"No."

"Bloody hell, Shrike. You need to tell me what happened."

"I don't know."

"You're a horrible liar. Where are you? I'll come to you."

Shrike clenched her jaw. "We're out of your jurisdiction."

"You murdered a man."

"He wasn't a man anymore." Shrike instantly regretted saying anything.

"You know who it was, don't you? Give me a name."

"I'm hanging up now and I'm blocking your number."

"Don't you dare."

"Let it go, Barsotti."

"Hanging up won't stop me from finding you and your siblings. It's just going to piss me off."

Shrike hung up and quickly turned her phone off. She didn't breathe until the screen went black.

"Anything we should worry about?" Wren asked.

"We were captured on the subway cameras. He knows."

"But," Lark said, "the suicide story."

"He's not buying it," Shrike said. "We can't go home. Not until Barsotti loses interest."

Lark shrunk back. "We don't have anywhere else to go."

"Well." Wren nervously cleared his throat. "I still have the list."

"The list?" Lark asked.

"The list of everyone we can remember saving. We can always check on the others."

"Kill them, you mean?" Shrike said.

"Well, I'm not saying that exactly—"

"No, I'm agreeing with you," Shrike said. "This is Dad's legacy we're talking about. I'm not okay with those things destroying his life's work."

"So we kill them all?" Lark said.

"We save the ones we have to the only way we can," Shrike said.

Wren nodded. "It's merciful, really."

"So we all agree?" Shrike waited for them each to nod. "Okay. Who do we check on first?"

"Wait." Lark's gaze flicked from the lookout to the neighboring trees that were teeming with winter birds. "This place is beautiful. Let's scatter Dad's ashes."

"Now?" Shrike asked.

"It seems long overdue," Wren said. "He deserves to rest."

"I'm not sure I'm ready to let him go," Shrike mumbled.

Both Wren and Lark reached for her hands, each taking one and giving it a squeeze. They sat quietly until she finally nodded.

"I'll go get him," Lark whispered.

Wren rubbed his thumb across her knuckles. It was a simple reminder that she wasn't alone, and it kept Shrike from breaking. Lark returned with the mud-stained box. Quietly, Shrike and Wren got up and followed Lark to a quiet spot by the lookout. Now that she was listening for it, she could catch the songs of a dozen different birds.

Cradling the box to her chest, Lark sniffed and looked at her siblings. "We should say something."

"Like what?" Shrike asked meekly.

"Okay, um." Lark licked her lips and lowered her gaze to the box. "I'm going to miss you, Daddy. And remember, you can come back and haunt me anytime. But don't worry about Shrike and Wren. I'll make sure they remember to laugh."

With a nod, she turned expectantly to Wren.

He cleared his throat. "Thanks, Dad. For everything. We were lucky to have you. I'll never be half the man you were, but I'll try to take care of them the way you would have wanted. And, you know, take better care of myself, too. You taught us well. We've got this."

Shrike felt their eyes on her but all she saw was that miserable little box.

"You deserved better," she said. "I should have been there to help you. I'll never forgive myself."

"Shrike," Wren whispered.

"I know he wouldn't want me to carry that guilt, but that doesn't change how I feel." Shaking her head, she wiped her eyes. "I promise you, Dad. I'll use it. Somehow, I'll let it make me a better person. I'm not exactly sure how I'll do that yet, but you know I'm not the brightest. And, I promise, if I can't figure it out, I'll let Wren and Lark help me."

"Who wants to do the honors?" Lark smiled sadly when neither of them replied. "Okay."

She walked to the very edge of the drop-off, ripped open the box, and carefully poured the ashes into the passing breeze. Shrike swallowed down the lump in her throat and lifted her gaze to the trees, watching the birds chirp and flutter about.

"He really would have liked this place," she whispered.

Lark's gasp drew Shrike's attention.

"Okay, don't be mad," Lark said as she rummaged in her pockets. "Dad sent me a sign, so I had to. And that makes it okay."

"What did you do?" Wren asked.

"Okay, we all agree that the pawnshop owner was lowballing us with Mom and Dad's rings, right? Well, while you and Shrike were haggling, Dad showed me these." She thrust her hand toward her siblings. Three pendants were nestled on her palm. Each of the small silver discs were embossed with a bright red cardinal.

"You stole those?" Shrike asked.

"Stole is a harsh word. I mean, can you steal your own property?"

"They weren't ours," Wren said.

"What are the odds that there would be *three* pendants all with Dad's favorite bird on them? Obviously, Dad wanted us to have them."

Shrike glanced to Wren. He shrugged and claimed one of the pendants, Shrike took another, and Lark cupped the last one to her chest.

"We should get going," Shrike said. "We really do need to get Wren that checkup. And the further we are from this city, the better."

Wren smiled at Lark. "You pick a direction and I'll pick a name?"

"All right." Lark shifted around nervously. "So, we're really doing this? We're going to kill them all?"

Shrike rubbed her thumb over the pendant, slowly tracing the outline of the cardinal. "Still breathing?"

\* \* \*

If you enjoyed the book, please leave a review. Your reviews inspire us to continue writing about the world of spooky and untold horrors!

Check out these best-selling books from our talented authors

### Ron Ripley (Ghost Stories)
- Berkley Street Series Books 1 – 9
  www.scarestreet.com/berkleyfullseries
- Moving in Series Box Set Books 1 – 6
  www.scarestreet.com/movinginboxfull

### A. I. Nasser (Supernatural Suspense)
- Slaughter Series Books 1 – 3 Bonus Edition
  www.scarestreet.com/slaughterseries

### David Longhorn (Sci-Fi Horror)
- Nightmare Series: Books 1 – 3
  www.scarestreet.com/nightmarebox
- Nightmare Series: Books 4 – 6
  www.scarestreet.com/nightmare4-6

### Sara Clancy (Supernatural Suspense)
- Banshee Series Books 1 – 6
  www.scarestreet.com/banshee1-6

For a complete list of our new releases and best-selling horror books, visit www.scarestreet.com/books


See you in the shadows,
Team Scare Street

Printed in Great Britain
by Amazon